SHEPHERD AND THE FOX

BRIAN SHEA

KRISTI BELCAMINO

SEVERN RIVER
PUBLISHING

Severn River Publishing
www.SevernRiverBooks.com

ISBN: 978-1-64875-253-7 (Paperback)

PROLOGUE

Kabul, Afghanistan

After the drone strike, people had fled screaming and crying from the alley where the small white van had been hit. A building struck by a second drone had been demolished, turning the alley into rubble.

While others ran away from the area, she ran toward it, glancing up at the sky.

"Incoming!" she screamed, face red, black eyes flashing.

Explosions rocked the air around her and yet she didn't flinch.

Sweat mixed with blood dripped down her face, seeping onto her flak jacket.

She swiped at it and then looked numbly at the blood.

It wasn't hers. A man around the corner had bled out a few seconds ago after she had briefly tried to stanch his wounds. They had been too great and she had been too late.

Now there was another man, this one very much alive, running straight into the area containing the remnants of the explosion . He was huge and muscular and wore a helmet and flak jacket.

"I heard there were children," he said in a deep voice.

She nodded despairingly and pointed, her manicured nails now black with dried blood.

A child's leg stuck out of the debris.

"No!" he shouted.

Then they both heard something and froze.

A child crying beneath a large pile of stones.

She dropped to her knees and frantically picked up large chunks of debris, chucking them behind her to unearth the child.

He did the same as he muttered, "Hang in there, buddy. We'll get you out."

After a few seconds, they'd cleared enough to see, miraculously, a small pocket within the rubble.

At first, she couldn't believe her eyes.

Four other children lay beneath the rubble.

She choked back a sob when she saw the crying child.

The little girl's brown hair was pulled back in a pink bow stained dark red. Her face was covered with blood and dirt. She couldn't have been older than three.

She stretched out her arms toward the woman.

But there was something heavy on the girl's foot. The woman tried to lift it but couldn't despite her grunting efforts.

"I got this," the man said, and with a loud groan, he lifted the heavy piece of concrete trapping the girl's foot.

The woman scooped the girl up in her arms and raced over to a bare patch of dirt.

She laid her down gently and began to tend to her wounds, checking the child for injuries.

The man had stayed behind to check for pulses on the other children.

When he walked over, she looked up. He sadly shook his head.

"You a doctor?" he asked.

She shook her head. "No."

"You seem to know what you're doing."

A strand of dark hair that had escaped her helmet hung in her face as she leaned over the child. "Trained EMT."

"How's she doing?"

"I stopped the bleeding but she's probably going to need surgery."

A siren wailed, and the man stood and shouted, "Over here! Help! Over here!"

A few seconds later, a team of medics swooped in and grabbed the girl, loading her onto a gurney.

"I'm coming with her," the woman said, helping to secure the child.

"We're airflighting her," one of the medics said. "No room."

"Roger that," she said.

As they carried the child away, she stood very still and watched.

Then she turned.

"That bomb killed at least seven children," she said to the man. "I saw three other bodies on the way in."

The man shook his head. "Damned Isis."

She opened her mouth to respond but an air siren drowned out her words.

The man looked at her and they both dove for cover in an open garage. They sat there for a few minutes.

"False alarm?" the man said.

"You never know around here."

Then it was quiet again. Sitting side by side, the man reached over, his hand covered in blood, and placed it on the woman's own bloody hand.

"Nice work back there," he said.

"Just doing my job."

"What is your job?"

"I'm just a volunteer." She looked away. "What about you?"

He opened his flak jacket and pointed to a patch of US flag.

"You're American?" He missed the danger in her voice.

"At your service."

She looked at him, her black eyes cold with fury.

"This is all your fault," she said, then jumped up and walked away.

He stared after her, his mouth open, speechless.

What the hell was she talking about?

Act I

1

_____

The Outskirts of Juarez

Rafael Dominguez sat in the windowless room chain-smoking Sobranie Black Russian cigarettes that had been proffered as a futile bribe the week before. He liked the taste of the cigarettes but thought the black and gold packaging was slightly garish.

His gray-streaked eyebrows knit together and his craggy, lined face was arranged in a frown as he examined the pack again, wondering idly what the cigarettes had cost. It didn't matter. He never took bribes. As head of security for the Orozco Cartel, he never wanted for anything.

His deadly reputation had even earned him a mention in a narcocor-rido ballad about Orozco Senior. The song, immediately banned from Mexican radio, had a line calling Dominguez the crazy son-of-a-bitch who executed the drug lord's enemies for him. It spoke about the hitman's lanky build and thick sideburns and his ability to beat any other gunman to the draw.

Now, Dominguez tapped his ash into the overflowing tray on the steel table and glanced around the room. He pushed back his thick, graying hair, hoping for a little relief from the oppressive heat.

He tugged at the collar of his beige button-down shirt and adjusted the crotch of his brown slacks. It was so hot in here even his balls were sweating. The room had a rusted fan in the corner that periodically emitted a pathetic squeak but offered zero relief as it half-heartedly circulated the sweat-permeated air.

His eyes fell on a small drop of dried blood on the corner of the table. He rubbed at it absentmindedly with his thumb, then met the eyes of his security guard posted by the door. The guard's eyes slid over to the bucket in the corner with the mop sticking out of it.

Dominguez followed his gaze. Drops of blood had dried on the outside of the bucket. He made a note to ensure whoever had cleaned up last time was given a warning. Just one.

With Orozco's father in charge, there would have been no warning.

But alas, things had changed.

Dominguez reached into an inside pocket of his checked sport coat and extracted a folded handkerchief. He neatly patted his brow where tiny beads of sweat had formed, then stubbed out one cigarette and lit another.

As he exhaled, the fresh plume of cigarette smoke swirled like a mini dust devil in the oppressive room.

Remaining expressionless, Dominguez glanced at his watch, even though it only confirmed what he knew: Carlos Machado, his counterpart for the Guzman Cartel, was late.

Counterpart was much too generous a word to describe Machado.

The younger man's reputation as a cocky, unpredictable, unhinged killer, combined with his tardiness to this meeting, made Dominguez wary.

The months of machinations leading up to the meeting were not something to take lightly. Today was the culmination of a loose pact between the two cartels that would serve to cement the financial futures of both organizations, not to mention their very survival.

To solidify the arrangement, Machado would personally deliver four hundred thousand dollars in cash to Dominguez.

For the most part, the two cartel leaders naturally stayed out of each other's way. Their business interests didn't often overlap.

Alejandro Guzman's realm was selling people. He'd been one of the first cartel leaders to mutate his drug business into one focused on human trafficking.

Sex trafficking of women and children, estimated to bring in more than one hundred and fifty billion dollars a year around the world, had quickly become a lucrative business for several Mexican cartels.

Orozco found the practice distasteful, but not enough to avoid forming an alliance with Guzman. Orozco simply considered himself more refined, preferring to stick to dealing drugs and guns.

To maintain his shaky moral ground, Orozco conveniently ignored the seedier ramifications of his business—such as teenage girls prostituting their bodies for drugs or addict mothers selling their children for drug money.

Now, Dominguez glanced at his watch. Again. The guard said something into his earpiece and nodded at Dominguez, who took out his cell phone and scrolled. He pulled up the security camera footage from the building's parking lot and watched Machado step out of a dusty Hummer with obnoxious orange rims. At least two men remained in the vehicle while two others flanked Machado as he strutted toward the front door. Both men wore bullet-proof vests over camouflage clothing and had AR-15 assault rifles slung across their torsos. Machado, small and wiry, wore an El Chapo-inspired silk paisley shirt with the collar unbuttoned, revealing thick gold chains and wiry chest hair.

None of the three men carried anything that could contain money, but Dominguez was not surprised. The money most likely remained in the Hummer.

Stopping in front of the door, Machado tilted his face up to the security camera, flashed a grin, and lifted a hand to wave.

Even on a small screen, Machado's energy was wired, manic, loco.

Dominguez's eyes narrowed as he examined Guzman's man.

Nobody had ever been a threat to Dominguez. But even so, a flicker of something unfamiliar trickled through him—unease. He quickly shook it off.

Dominguez put down his phone, met the eyes of his security guard, and gave a slight nod.

The guard spoke into the headset in a low voice. After a few seconds, he nodded at Dominguez.

The door to the room opened and Machado stood there with a cocky grin.

"Amigo!" he said, spreading his arms wide in greeting.

Dominguez didn't respond. He eyed the younger man, taking him in from head to toe, and then gave a nod.

Machado's security men stood behind him, forming a human wall.

Dominguez cocked a thick eyebrow and jutted his chin at the men.

"They wait outside. These were not the terms of our meeting."

Machado's tongue ran over his front teeth as he eyed the older man. Then, with a shrug, he smiled and said, "No problemo, my friend. My men will wait in the hall with your man."

Machado gave a meaningful glance to the security guard inside the room.

"He will remain in the room with us," Dominguez said firmly.

"I don't think so." Machado cocked an eyebrow.

"He is unarmed."

Machado's mouth spread into a wolfish grin.

"We'll see about that." He nodded, and one of his men entered the room and patted the guard down. Then the man nodded at Machado and exited.

"Satisfied?" Dominguez asked.

Machado didn't answer, instead striding toward the middle of the room.

The guard closed the door behind him.

Nodding at the metal chair across from him, Dominguez said, "Please have a seat."

Crossing his arms, Machado leaned against one water-stained concrete wall. "Thanks, old man, but I'll stand."

Without reacting to the insult, Dominguez lit another cigarette. He inhaled deeply and exhaled before he looked up at the younger man and held out his pack of cigarettes.

"I only vape," Machado said. "Better for the lungs."

Dominguez gave a slight nod.

"As you might have realized, we do things a little differently than Guzman," he said. "In the future, to show your respect for our arrangement, I'm going to insist that you be on time."

"You insist?" Machado cackled. "Sure, yeah, whatever you say."

Machado reached inside his shirt pocket and extracted a toothpick. He stuck it in his teeth and then began to play with it with his tongue, keeping his eyes trained on Dominguez.

Unruffled, Dominguez continued. "Preparedness and punctuality are two of the most important qualities of a leader. It shows that you respect your commitments. It would be in your best interest to adhere to what you might consider an old-fashioned sign of respect."

Machado spat on the floor and ran his tongue around the inside of his mouth again. After giving the guard a withering glance, Machado laughed again.

"Don't talk to me about respect, old man. You better watch how you speak to me. Guzman insists you show me respect or we will have a problem."

He sneered as he emphasized the word "insists."

It was becoming clear that things could go sideways at any second. Dominguez resisted the urge to glance at his phone to see what was going on in the hallway outside the door.

"Enough of this talk for now," he said lightly. "Please instruct your men to place the money in the SUV parked outside. Once they have done so, they can drive to the end of the road. We will count the money. Once we are satisfied, we will escort you to where they are waiting."

Machado flicked the toothpick around his mouth with his tongue. He didn't answer.

The alarms in Dominguez's head grew louder.

"See, that's the thing," Machado said. "I didn't bring any money."

Dominguez felt his body tense. He again resisted glancing at his phone.

"I'm here to relay a message from Guzman," Machado said. "We don't really see the benefit in an arrangement with you."

We. Dominguez would never have spoken for Orozco in that way.

"I think you should reconsider," he said, then took his time lighting another cigarette before continuing. "This arrangement will secure the financial future for both of our cartels. This deal means everyone involved will be wealthy beyond belief."

Machado laughed. "Guzman doesn't need your money. We're pulling out of the deal, old man. You can waste your breath trying to talk us out of it, but nothing you can say will change that. Guzman doesn't need you. Just face that reality. Your time is over. You might have once been something, but now you're old and worn out. A has-been."

Dominguez was dangerously motionless, the cigarette in his hand forgotten, the ash so long it dropped onto the steel table.

For a second, something primitive and uneasy flickered over Machado's face, but then his bravado returned. He clapped his hands together.

"So, my job here is done. I guess Guzman must have enough respect for you to tell you in person. If it were up to me, I wouldn't have done even that."

Dominguez held up his hand.

"One moment," he said, and reached for his phone. "I'll see if Orozco has a message to send back to Guzman."

"Whatever." Machado pulled the chair toward him, flipping it around and sitting backward on it. He leaned forward and grinned at Dominguez, who was squinting and typing on his phone. A few seconds later, the phone buzzed.

Dominguez looked at the phone and then glanced at the guard.

The guard said something into his headset and then reached over to lock the door.

Machado sprang to his feet.

"What the hell?"

He glanced wildly between Dominguez and the guard.

"If you don't unlock the door right now, you're a dead man. Guzman said if you showed the slightest disrespect for me, it would be all-out war."

Dominguez glanced at the guard, who nodded at something being said into his earpiece.

Panic spread across Machado's face. He stood and pointed at Dominguez, his hand shaking.

"Unlock the door! If I don't walk out of here right now, my men are going to massacre every last person in this place. And then we will go after all of your family members and hang them from the trees of plaza de armas for the world to see." Dominguez, who had just looked at his phone, set it down and stared at Machado for a long second. Then he smiled and shrugged, nodding at the guard to unlock the door. Machado grinned and began to walk toward the door but then jumped back in horror. The two bloody heads of Machado's security guards rolled through the open doorway like bowling balls. One of them came to a stop, resting near the tip of Machado's fancy snakeskin cowboy boots.

The door slammed shut again.

"Take a seat," Dominguez said.

Ashen-faced, Machado did so.

"As I mentioned earlier, punctuality is not actually about being on time. It's about following through on your commitments. For instance, when I agree to something—anything—I follow through. It could be as simple as being home for dinner on time. Or as large as following through on a business deal such as we had. It's all a matter of integrity."

He paused.

Machado's eyes were wild now, roaming the nearly empty room, fruitlessly looking for a way to escape. Sweat had now stained the armpits of his silk shirt.

"I can try to get Guzman to reconsider," Machado said in a wobbly voice.

Instead of answering, Dominguez leaned over and held out his cigarette pack. This time Machado took one. He picked up the lighter and leaned forward to light the cigarette.

"Do you understand now why being punctual is important?" Dominguez asked, exhaling a plume of smoke. "How you spend your time matters. We are all given the same twenty-four hours each day. The ones who are most successful in this life use their time wisely. You can make your time feel short or long, depending."

Dominguez then lit his own cigarette before nodding at the security guard, who left his post and headed toward Machado.

"For instance," Dominguez said, "how long do you think the last few seconds of your life will feel?"

2

Campestre Juarez Country Club

Lucky paused in the ballroom doorway and shook her long dark hair over her shoulders one more time. She pressed her curvy red lips together and lowered her eyelashes in a seemingly modest move that was actually a calculated maneuver to scan the room.

Massive chandeliers sparkled overhead, casting the room in a magical glow. Waiters in black carried silver trays with champagne and caviar nestled on small, crisp toasts. Women adorned in festive dresses—pink taffeta, red sequins, yellow silks—carried Louis Vuittons and Hermès and Birkin bags.

The air was filled with the tinkling of crystal glasses and laughter and loud boasting from the pot-bellied men in their tuxedos.

Seeing all the women dressed in bright colors assured Lucky that she'd chosen an outfit that would make her stand out—a form-fitting black dress that hugged every curve and fell in a silky puddle to the floor. The back was nonexistent. Instead of wearing the yellow diamond on its long pendant against her bodice, she wore the necklace backward so the glimmering jewel sat nestled between her two delicate shoulder blades.

At first glance, she looked underdressed, but the women in the room had a discerning eye and they would immediately register the necklace, the seven-thousand-dollar Oscar de la Renta dress, and the small, diamond-encrusted clutch she held.

Her ridiculously expensive outfit would ensure her acceptance into the elite world of Juarez's rich and famous. This was a night to make friends and garner attention, and extract crucial information from important people.

It had started last week when she moved into one of the most ostentatious houses in the ritzy Campestre neighborhood—a swanky mansion with gold front doors, palatial ceilings, and a pool with a waterfall.

Although she'd had the se venta—for sale—sign removed, nobody needed to know that she was just renting. She'd made sure that everyone who was anyone in Juarez had heard the tale about a rich heiress named Eve Rodriguez walking into the mortgage company and plunking down fat stacks of cash. The lender had agreed to pocket one thick stack and tell anyone who asked that she was the owner, not a renter.

The Campestre enclave was where all of Juarez's wealthy citizens lived. After a ten-year period where people had fled the lavish neighborhood because of cartel violence, the area was having a comeback, and vacant houses were quickly being purchased. Now the driveways and garages were filled with BMWs and Lexuses and Range Rovers.

Paying cash for an annual membership at the country club had cemented her place in high society. Now she just had a few points to fine tune and she'd get what she came for.

That morning at the golf course had gone as planned. She'd sidled up to the mayor in her tight turquoise silk golfing pants to ask his advice on which club to use.

When he'd found out she was new to town, he'd chivalrously offered to escort her home "to get her there safely."

She'd agreed, and he'd rubbed his meaty hands together in anticipation until he realized her two silent bodyguards would be along for the ride.

"I'm sorry," she said. "I just remembered that my father is expecting a call from me. I must do it in the privacy of my car. Maybe another time?"

A group of women, including the mayor's wife, had just entered the courtyard from the tennis courts. He was growing visibly uncomfortable and kept casting glances behind him when Lucky said, "Maybe we could get together tonight? It's been so hard to meet people here. You've been the only one who has been kind to me all week."

At first the mayor's face fell. "I have plans tonight."

Lucky pouted her pink-painted lips.

Behind him, the women had disappeared into the country club's bar.

Seeing this, the mayor smiled and turned back toward Lucky, snapping his fingers.

"I have an idea! You can come along tonight."

"Really? Where?"

"It's a cocktail party—here at the club," he offered. "Have you not received an invite?"

Lucky frowned and shook her head. "No, should I have?"

"Yes!" The mayor gave her a benevolent smile. "Consider this your formal invitation. What kind of mayor would I be if I didn't take care of our newest residents?"

Lucky breathed a loud sigh of relief. "Thank you. I was dreading being home alone again tonight."

"One thing," the mayor said, casting a disparaging glance at the bodyguards. "Because Campestre Country Club is a gated community and we have our own security, it won't be necessary for you to bring your security guards tonight. I'd be happy to escort you home."

Lucky gave a wide smile. "Wonderful. See you tonight."

Now, paused in the ballroom doorway, eyes hooded, she quickly scanned the crowd to clock the key players. The mayor, her first target, was at one o'clock. His reputation as a ladies' man made him the easiest to infiltrate, and it looked like he was already six sheets to the wind. The former assistant bank manager was at four o'clock. Lucky would make sure the mayor introduced them within the next ten minutes. The current bank manager's wife was in the corner. She'd be optional. The cartel head and his cunning wife were at eight o'clock. She'd do her best to avoid them while also making sure they noticed her.

Taking a deep breath and throwing her shoulders back, Lucky stepped into the room.

A path cleared and admiring glances followed her as she strode through the crowd, her eyes locked on the mayor.

3

A flashing neon sign from the bodega across the street lit up the entire studio apartment, which wasn't much bigger than the full-size bed Shepherd was lying in. The air was hot and sticky, not even the faintest breeze entering the room's open window.

Staring up at the fan slowly circulating above the bed, Shepherd was mesmerized by the movement and quickly found himself swept away in a dark memory involving helicopter blades, shouting, gunfire, and bloodshed.

Naked and on top of the sheets, he didn't bother swiping at the rivulets of sweat sliding off his temple and snaking down the side of his bald head to the already damp sheet. Solimar stirred beside him, making a soft, sexy sound in her sleep.

Shepherd startled as the blaring sound of Tamborazo Zacatecano music erupted from the house across the street. Seconds later, as if on cue, the downstairs neighbors turned on their music.

Ten o'clock. Siesta was over. Time to sing and dance and eat and drink mas cervezas.

Across the neighborhood, impressive sound systems erupted, adding to the nightly cacophony.

Solimar, still asleep beside him, was used to the nightly symphony and didn't stir. He'd been living there for two months but hadn't yet grown accustomed to the nightly alarm clock.

Shepherd sat up and reached over to the kitchen table, only a few inches away, plucking a gallon of water off of it.

Another four gallons sat on the floor beside a small, freestanding structure that contained the kitchen sink beside two built-in burners. All of Solimar's cooking utensils and pantry items were stored in one of the cupboards underneath the sink. A shelf above the sink held a neat stack of colorful bowls and plates that stood out against this wall, which was painted bright pink but appeared orange in the flashing neon lights.

Shepherd pulled himself to a sitting position, nearly knocking the wooden cross off the wall beside him, and gulped down some of the water.

He moved gingerly, but Solimar still uttered a soft, mumbled complaint. Because he was such a big man, the entire bed rocked with his slightest movement.

Standing a good five inches over six feet, Shepherd packed 260 pounds of nearly pure muscle on his frame. His muscular neck and well-shaped bald head were softened by warm brown eyes and an undeniably sexy smile.

As the son of a Hawaiian woman and African-American man, his skin was the bronze color of a Saint-Tropez tan and made his perfect white-toothed grin even more appealing when he chose to flash it.

When he was a pre-teen, an early predisposition to chunkiness and some of the teasing that went along with it had sent Shepherd to the gym every day after school, where he quickly found that he was naturally stronger than any other boy in his grade and older.

Now, at thirty-five, he was in his prime and could bench press a grizzly bear if he felt like it.

The circumference of his biceps was nearly as large as the curvy Solimar's waist.

She had once unfurled a faded tape measure to prove it. Her waist came in at twenty-seven inches. His biceps spanned an impressive twenty-three.

For fun, she measured her breasts and hips and declared that according to science, she had the perfect body.

"No argument there," he'd said, and gave her a slow smile.

They'd had some fun in this fourth-floor walkup. The entire floor shared a rusty bathroom at the far end.

Solimar often watched him when he stripped down in the studio apartment's sultry air and wore only a towel wrapped around his waist to go to the bathroom down the hall.

A woman who lived in an apartment nearby once stood naked in the open doorway as he passed, leering at him. Seeing this, Solimar flew into a rage and nearly scratched the woman's eyes out before Shepherd lifted her into the air and carried her back to her place.

Now, remembering her fiery temper, he grinned. Then he jumped as his phone buzzed on the kitchen table. He snatched up the phone. Only one person had his number.

His face remained emotionless as he read the text:

It's go time.

The call he'd been waiting on for the past two months.

Without a word, he stood and pulled on his pants and shirt, then walked over to a hook on the door and reached for his jacket. He lifted a 9 mm Glock G17 off the kitchen table and tucked it into his waistband at the small of his back before opening his wallet and taking out a stack of bills. He placed the money on the table where the gun had been before turning toward the door.

As soon as his palm cupped the door, he was slammed into it. He recovered and turned to see Solimar standing there naked, her legs spread, her eyes flashing dangerously as she swore at him in Spanish and threw the stack of money at his head. It bounced off his cheek.

"You dare treat me like a whore? You dare to give me money after all the time we spent together? And you think five hundred dollars is what I charge. Ha! If I charged, you would not be able to afford me!" Her words were pure venom. "You are a coward, sneaking off in the night!"

"It's not like that," he said in a calm voice. "I thought maybe it would help with the rent since I won't be around to pay half."

He leaned down patiently and plucked the money off the ground, holding it out to her.

"I told you this would happen. I warned you I would have to leave one day."

"In the middle of the night?" she asked. Her eyes blazed with fury and suspicion.

He nodded.

"What are you? A spy? CIA? Undercover cop? Homeland security?"

He squinted as he looked down at her. "Something like that."

She swatted his hand and the money went flying again.

He didn't move this time.

She stared at him for a long moment.

"It's her," she finally said.

"What?" His brow furrowed.

"I always knew there was someone else," she said. "That's why you never gave yourself to me."

"What?" he said again. "This is strictly business."

She sighed and shook her head, opening the door for him.

"I don't believe you. I just hope she's worth it."

He walked out without answering.

4

Downtown Juarez at Night
Deadliest City in the World

Some said that the murder sprees between rival cartels only ceased when the Mexican national football team was playing.

Tonight was not a game night.

Shepherd walked down the darkened back streets and alleys of Juarez, an imposing silhouette of pure sinew and muscle. Small groups of drug dealers on corners backed away as he passed. Even the braver prostitutes on the street corners eyed him and then whispered among themselves without approaching him. It was more than his size and bulk alone. Tonight, there was an aura about him that sent fear spiking through those who saw him.

Only when he saw a fluffy cat and reached down to stroke its fur did his smile erupt into an expression that inevitably disarmed everyone. The entire block seemed to expel a collective sigh of relief.

A few blocks later, Shepherd strode past an active crime scene—not that unusual for night time in Juarez.

Federal police stood on the corner holding automatic rifles next to a black truck with flashing lights. A man in a white hazmat suit unfurled a long strip of red crime scene tape that said "Peligro" across an alley entryway already marked off with the traditional yellow tape. A small group of investigators stood nearby. Their words floated on the air as he passed, and Shepherd caught snatches of them. "Kidnapped from El Paso. Cartel. Message."

He glanced over and saw the body near a brick wall, uncovered and open to the sticky night air. The man's hands were cut off and resting on his bare chest near a large tattoo of the Virgin de Guadalupe. His jeans were pulled down to his ankles in a final indignity.

Shepherd kept walking.

The air was filled with the familiar sounds of Narco music. Strains of cowboy ballads praising drug lords filtered out from the graffiti-covered apartment buildings he passed. Black iron bars covered windows and front doors, and stucco was peeling off most buildings.

He entered a livelier business district in the city center and crossed the street toward a bodega. He strode inside and passed two old men playing chess at a small table in the corner. A group stood around the table, commenting on the game.

"Queen to Rook 5 mate," Shepherd said as he passed.

The crowd erupted in cheers as the move was made and resulted in a checkmate.

He didn't pause as he made his way toward the back of the store. The clerk behind the counter eyed him but didn't say a word. Shepherd passed through a door that said "Employees Only" in Spanish and headed straight to a large steel freezer door. A man with an assault rifle slung over his chest stood in front of it.

"I need to see Fast Eddie," Shepherd said.

The guard shook his head. "He's busy."

"Tell him I'm here," Shepherd said firmly.

The men exchanged a long look and the guard said something into his shoulder microphone. Then he looked back up.

"Like I said, he's in the middle of something."

The look Shepherd gave the guard would make a smaller or unarmed man run for the hills.

The guard shifted and Shepherd saw a retinal scanner lock on the door behind him.

"I need to see Fast Eddie," Shepherd repeated in a calm voice, a dangerous glint in his eyes. "I don't want any trouble."

The guard stared at Shepherd, cracking his knuckles, then shrugged and said, "Your funeral, *pendejo*."

A few seconds later, the steel door behind the man swung open and Fast Eddie whirled around. Shepherd stood there holding the limp body of the guard whose face was pressed up against the retinal scanner.

Shepherd dropped the unconscious man to the ground and stepped inside the room.

Fast Eddie gave an impish grin, his arched eyebrows and elongated mouth reminiscent of a circus clown.

He clapped his hands together.

"Come in! Come in! I didn't know it was you. Why didn't you say so?"

Shepherd didn't answer, just looked over at the bank of security camera monitors that showed every inch of the bodega, including the room right outside the door.

"I need those, um, supplies I mentioned."

"Now? Are you loco? It's the middle of the night." Fast Eddie laughed, spreading his arms wide and shrugging.

"I gave you two months to get them for me. I told you to have them ready."

"It's not easy to find those types of weapons without arousing suspicion. I ran into some difficulties." Fast Eddie gave him a toothy grin.

Shepherd looked back at the guard on the ground.

"That guy ran into some difficulties, too. And look what happened to him."

Fast Eddie's face drained of color. He took a step back, putting his palms up. "Okay. Okay. I can give you what I have from my personal stash. It will take me a few hours."

"I need them now."

Shepherd moved closer. Fast Eddie backed up. Shepherd took another step. Fast Eddie was now backed into a corner.

"It's all in the back. I can take you there now."

"Aha," Shepherd said, and gave the other man a slap on the shoulder. "Now we're getting somewhere. I can do without some of my order, but I'm going to need the Brugger and Thomet MP9 for sure."

Fast Eddie scratched his head, his face scrunched up. He spread his arms wide, palms up. "See, there's a problem."

"A problem?" Shepherd tilted his head. "What sort of problem?"

"Someone else bought it." Fast Eddie looked down at his feet as he spoke.

"Someone else?" Shepherd's voice was a low growl. "I must have heard you wrong. You didn't just say that someone else bought the Brugger and Thomet MP9 I paid you cash for two months ago?"

Shepherd folded his arms across his chest and shook his head. "Go get the rest of it. Now!"

Armed with a bullet-proof vest, night vision goggles, and an extra Glock, Shepherd left out the bodega's back door. He was still fuming that Fast Eddie had sold someone else the submachine gun he'd paid for, but was trying to let it go. He'd deal with Fast Eddie another time. Right now, he had to concentrate on his mission—to provide additional security for a hit team going into the only bank in Juarez controlled by the cartel.

He had a long night ahead of him so when he passed a man in the entrance of an alley grabbing a woman's arm, he mentally cringed but figured it was none of his business.

But then the woman's cries grew louder and he heard the crash of metal trash cans.

He turned to see the man had picked up the woman and pressed her against the alley wall, her dress ripped down the middle. He had one hand over the woman's mouth, pressing her head against the alley wall, while the other hand unbuttoned his pants.

Shepherd grabbed the guy by the back of his collar and flung him across the alley, where he bounced off the concrete wall and landed on the ground. The man tried to get up but Shepherd's fist sent him flying back down to the ground.

Shepherd towered over him.

"You ever do something like that again to a woman, I will hunt you down and strip the flesh off your body."

The man spat out blood and then swore, trying to sit up.

Shepherd was about to place one steel-toe boot on the man's chest to prove his point when the woman came up from behind and, in one swift motion, sliced the man's neck with a broken bottle.

For a second, Shepherd and the woman stood there, watching the blood pour onto the concrete as the man died. Then Shepherd turned to look at her. A light from a neon sign illuminated her face. She had porcelain skin, curly black hair, and huge black eyes. She looked like a doll. She was panting heavily and tears slid down her cheeks.

"You okay?" he said.

"He raped me last week. He was going to do it again."

Shepherd gave a slow nod. They heard voices behind them and whirled around to find a group of people talking loudly and growing closer.

"Go," Shepherd said. "Run that way. I'll make sure nobody comes down this alley until you're in the clear."

After looking up at him for a long second, the woman nodded and ran.

Shepherd came stumbling out of the alley, pretending to be drunk.

The group laughed at him and he joined them, singing loudly in Spanish. After a few blocks, he peeled off in another direction.

5

Juarez's bustling city center was just starting to awaken.

Shop owners were unlocking businesses up and down the area's main street—Avenida 16 de Septiembre.

Shepherd, seated at a sidewalk café table, had his long legs sprawled partially into the walkway. He was drinking black coffee and contemplating a chessboard on the table before him.

An older man sat across from him. Bright blue eyes squinted out of tan, leathery skin as the man peered down at the chessboard. His shoulder-length hair was pushed back from his forehead and fell in waves along each side of his face. His bushy eyebrows were still dark even though his hair and neatly trimmed beard had grayed.

Several blocks away, the street ended at Our Lady of Guadalupe Cathedral and the town square, the plaza de armas—Weapons Square.

As the sky erupted into brilliant pink and gold, the lights illuminating the cathedral's looming bell towers flickered off.

Shepherd plucked his black knight and plopped it down with a thud. "Check."

"You sure you want to do that?" Red asked.

He spoke slowly in a deep, gravelly voice, choosing his words carefully.

"Damn it," Shepherd said. "What do you see that I don't?" He leaned over the board. "As far as I can tell, you're going to lose your rook no matter what you do."

Red smiled and then moved his king out of harm's way.

Within seconds, Shepherd had taken the rook, but then immediately saw his mistake. Red moved a bishop the length of the board, effectively trapping Shepherd's king.

"Checkmate."

Shepherd frowned and pushed himself back from the table.

"Don't take it so hard," Red said, and chuckled. "I got lucky."

Shepherd frowned and shot him a look. "Not funny."

"Sorry. My bad."

Both men looked up as a car slowed down near the alley across the street but then kept going.

"You see what I did?" Red asked.

"Yeah, you won," Shepherd said drily.

"What I did was distract you. I baited you. I offered up my rook knowing it wouldn't matter if I lost it because I was about to checkmate you."

Shepherd just shook his head.

Red looked down the sidewalk past Shepherd.

"Watch out for this yahoo," he said. They both turned to watch a man walk unsteadily toward them, sporting a cowboy hat and guitar slung across his chest.

Shepherd drew in his long legs to make room for the careening man.

"Must've been a really good party," he said.

Red chuckled. "Obviously the party is still going on for this fellow."

After he passed, Shepherd jutted his chin toward the bank across the street as a man in a three-piece suit approached the front door. He and Red silently watched as the man unlocked the front door and then held it open as an elderly woman approached the bank.

The two exchanged words as the man's eyes traveled up and down the street before he stepped inside. By the time his gaze had roamed over the café, Red and Shepherd were already bent over, intensely concentrating on the chessboard.

The men were deep into another chess game before the street fully came to life. The sidewalks now bustled with people. Smells of pan dulce and hot cakes con tocino filled the air. Groups of people stood in line at the market waiting for it to open for the day. An employee at Domino's Pizza turned on its open sign at the same time the owner of a smoke shop came out to sweep the sidewalk.

At the end of the street, at the plaza de armas, vendors set up their goods under red and white striped canopies and crowds began milling about the plaza examining the wares on offer.

Without turning their heads, both men registered a beat-up Chevy pulling into a bank employee parking lot in the adjacent alley.

Shepherd took a last pull of his coffee, then stood and left without a word.

The driver was a large man with a massive beer belly, and by the time he emerged from his vehicle in a wrinkled security guard uniform, Shepherd was on him.

As the driver reached to get an insulated lunch bag out of the back seat, Shepherd looped a large forearm around his neck in an expert chokehold. Within seconds, the man was slumped in Shepherd's arms.

Dragging the unconscious man along with him, Shepherd kicked the car door closed and ducked into an alcove.

In the privacy of the dark alcove, Shepherd stripped the guard down. Then, in a swift, practiced move, he ripped the Velcroed front of his pants and they fell off. Within seconds, Shepherd was in the guard's uniform and dragging the boxer-clad man toward a rusted green pickup that had just turned down the alley.

Red rolled down the pickup's window, his gray mustache twisted in a wry grin.

"Nice outfit."

The sleeves on the guard's gray uniform didn't even reach Shepherd's forearms and the pants swum high above his ankles.

"Yuck it up," Shepherd said.

Red leaped out of the truck and pulled down the tailgate before helping Shepherd haul the large man into the bed.

Moments later, Red was driving away and Shepherd was heading to the bank, tugging futilely at the uniform's too-tight crotch area.

The whole operation took less than five minutes.

As Shepherd rounded the corner, he didn't flinch upon seeing the two police officers leaning against their squad car, smoking and drinking coffee.

Both officers gave him the once-over.

One of them made a crack in Spanish about Shepherd looking like a schoolboy who hadn't been allowed to wear long pants yet.

Shepherd gave an apologetic shrug and mumbled something about too many tamales but kept walking. He was right at the bank entrance, about to pull open the door, when one of the officers pushed himself off the car and said in Spanish, "You new? Where's Enrique?"

Shepherd stopped with his back to the officers; his hand dropped to his side, closer to his concealed weapon.

His entire body tensed, fingers flexing, as he remained frozen, waiting.

Suddenly, the street behind the men erupted in a cacophony of blaring horns, people swearing and shouting, and brakes squealing.

Out of the corner of his eye, Shepherd noted the stretch limousine that had come to a stop in the middle of the street.

The limo had stopped traffic on both sides of the busy street, and all activity on the bustling sidewalks stopped. As everyone in the area turned to look at the limo, including the cops, Shepherd ripped open the bank door and slipped inside.

6

The honking and shouting immediately ceased as Lucia "Lucky" Evelyn Rodriguez-Toscani extended one stiletto-clad foot out the stretch limousine's open door.

The street seemed to hold its breath as she took the proffered hand of one of her heavily armed bodyguards. She emerged from the vehicle and paused dramatically between her two bodyguards before taking her first step toward the bank.

She tossed her long dark hair, her eyes hidden behind oversized sunglasses, full lips painted blood red, and a duffle-sized Balenciaga bag casually slung over one shoulder.

She wore nothing under the Versace Medusa leather blazer, revealing a generous eyeful of cleavage laden with a thick tangle of gold necklaces. She hugged a fluffy white Pomeranian to her side with a hand dripping in gold and diamond rings.

A man walking on the opposite sidewalk was so enraptured by the vision of Lucky emerging from the limousine that he slammed right into a telephone pole, spilling his armload of produce.

Lucky entered the bank, her red-soled Christian Louboutin heels clicking and clacking before she paused dramatically on the marble floor in the center of the lobby.

Behind her dark Gucci sunglasses, she was methodically clocking the lobby's occupants. All heads turned to watch as she entered, except one. She caught a glimpse of a man's shoulder as he turned away, but his head was hidden by a thick pillar. A flicker of annoyance thrummed through her. She didn't like walking into a job and having any unknowns—even a man whose face she couldn't see.

She ignored the feeling and, adopting an air of privilege and impatience, lifted her hand and crooked a finger, summoning a bank employee from a nearby desk.

The man tugged at his shirt collar as he made his way over to Lucky. He was tall and thin with prematurely thinning black hair and a large, hooked nose.

"I need to see the manager," she said in a husky voice that left no room for argument. "Now."

A flush crept up the man's neck as he stammered, "He's, um, busy. I can help you."

Lucky gave a slight, dangerous shake of her head.

"Maybe you didn't hear me. I need to see the manager. Now."

As the teller opened his mouth to protest, Lucky leaned over and put one red-painted fingernail against his lips, shaking her head.

"Shhh," she said. "I bet you like your job here, don't you?"

The teller nodded, wide-eyed.

"Then you need to get the manager or you won't be working here by the close of business, understood?"

The teller turned his head and made eye contact with a man in a corner office. The man looked up from his desk and gave a quick shake of his head, but Lucky had already seen him. Her lips curled into a smile.

"Good boy," she said to the teller, and turned toward the manager's office.

The manager, a squat, balding man stuffed into a three-piece navy suit, gave Lucky a nod and stepped out of his office.

As he grew closer and took in her appearance, she could see the annoyance on his face soften.

Under hooded eyes, the manager looked Lucky up and down. She knew he was a numbers guy and was silently calculating the worth of her clothing, jewelry, and accessories.

By the time he reached her side, he waved the younger man away and was prepared to grovel for this woman's business.

"I'm so sorry you had to bother with him," the manager said. Then he paused. "Have we met?"

Lucky lifted her sunglasses off her eyes for a second and smiled.

The bank manager snapped his fingers. "You were at the cocktail party last night at the country club."

"Bingo!" Lucky smiled.

"What can I help you with ... Miss?"

Lucky gave him an indulgent smile and ignored his graceless attempt to finagle her name.

"I'm looking for a bank where my money will be safe," she said.

A wide smile spread across the manager's face.

"Step this way," he said, and began leading her toward his office. "You've definitely come to the right place. This bank is the safest in all of Mexico."

Lucky's expression showed she was not convinced. "I have a rather large inheritance that I need to deposit into a bank I can trust."

"How large?" the manager asked.

Lucky paused in front of a desk. She leaned over and plucked a pen out of the startled employee's hand and scribbled on a piece of paper.

The manager leaned over to read the number she had written—twenty-six million dollars.

His eyes grew wide and he swallowed. "Please follow me to my office so that we can discuss how best to serve you, Miss...?"

"Miss is fine," Lucky said in a haughty tone. "I still have not decided if your bank is suitable for me and my money."

Her glance roamed dismissively over the teller, who was looking at the floor.

"This way, please," the manager said.

"Show me where the vault is. If it's not secure enough, this conversation is over," Lucky said.

The manager nodded. "I can show you the outside."

"Fine."

With her two bodyguards trailing a few feet behind, Lucky followed him toward a thick oak door leading to a long hallway. The door was open and two security guards stood just inside the hallway, each wearing pistols in hip holsters. They straightened a little as Lucky and the manager stepped past them. The manager stopped and turned toward Lucky.

"Your men will have to wait here."

Lucky shook her head. "These are my most trusted men. My father has ordered them to never leave my side."

She leaned close, exposing the manager to her ample cleavage and a whiff of her spicy perfume. "Juarez is a dangerous place under any circumstances, but even more so when money is involved."

The bank manager's certainty faltered a bit, and he stammered before mumbling, "It's bank policy. My apologies."

Lucky straightened and looked at her bodyguards, who stood on the other side of the two security guards. The four men were eyeballing each other. But unlike her men, who were expert mercenaries, the two bank employees were older, overweight, and probably underpaid.

With a nonchalant shrug, Lucky opened her Balenciaga tote.

"I was worried you might say that," she said, and in the blink of an eye, lifted a Brügger & Thomet MP9 out of the bag and jammed it under the bank manager's chin.

"I don't understand!" he said, his eyes wide with shock.

At the same time, her bodyguards stuck guns to the security guards' heads. They both immediately thrust their hands in the air and muttered, "*No problemo, no problemo.*"

With a start, Lucky realized that right before she'd jammed her weapon into the manager's wobbly flesh, he had reached out to push a small, clear button on the wall.

A silent alarm.

Lucky's eyes flashed. Game on.

She turned toward the bank lobby, knowing exactly what type of shitstorm was headed her way.

"*Attencion!*" she shouted to the bystanders in Spanish. "This is a robbery! I'll give you thirty seconds to get out of here before I start shooting!"

People stood stunned for a second, staring at her, not comprehending her words.

"Didn't you hear me? Leave! Now!" she shouted, and moved the gun away from the bank manager's jaw to fire a shot into the ceiling.

That worked.

People screamed and raced for the exit in a fury. Lucky grinned at the manager. "Sometimes actions speak louder than words."

Sweat poured down the man's face.

Lucky pointed the gun at him with one hand and clutched the Pomeranian with the other.

She leaned down and kissed the top of the dog's head, keeping her eyes on the bank manager.

"Sorry if that scared you, sweetie," she said to the dog.

7

After jamming her weapon back into the manager's fleshy neck, Lucky was about to turn toward the back of the bank when a volley of gunfire erupted and the large windows disintegrated in a cascade of tinkling glass and piercing screams.

From her vantage point, Lucky could see her driver crouching near the limousine's back fender. He was in the thick of a vicious gun battle with the two police officers stationed outside the bank. They'd made their way up the steps and were now turned around, shooting at Lucky's driver.

The driver had given her a few extra seconds. With dismay, Lucky saw another squad car pull up in the street. Police from that vehicle ran toward the bank. One snuck up on her driver from behind and ended the shootout with a precision headshot. Lucky flinched as he collapsed onto the ground.

As the officers stormed the entrance, paving their way with a hail of bullets, Lucky's bodyguards released the security guards and moved in unison to stand in front of her, letting loose a flurry of bullets.

Once the guns had been removed from their heads, the security guards fled out a side door, leaving the manager sputtering in fear and fury.

The cops inside the bank were obviously cartel cops, on the payroll to protect Orozco's money, not the citizens of Juarez. They fired wildly with little disregard for the few people still inside the bank. An elderly woman in a floral house dress dove to the ground and then executed an impressive series of rolls toward one wall. A young man army-crawled behind one of the lobby's large wooden desks. A mother with a toddler huddled in the corner, shaking.

Meanwhile, Lucky's bodyguards methodically ducked and rolled, evading bullets only to come up and fire at the four cartel cops.

Lucky was partially tucked behind the hallway's large, thick door, which provided a modicum of protection for her. However, with her gun shoved up in the bank manager's business and her grip on the Pomeranian, she was unable to help her bodyguards in their battle against the police.

Outside, the street rumbled as more cartel forces arrived. A large narco tank—a modified semi-truck cab plated with steel armor—skidded to a stop in front of the bank. Four men wearing A-15 rifles and camouflage leaped out and raced up the steps.

Cartel hitmen.

Lucky, who had shed the rich bitch act and was now cool and methodical in her every movement, saw the Hummer and its crew arrive and calmly pushed the bank manager deeper down the hallway.

Lucky's bodyguards unloaded on the approaching cartel members, sending plaster shrapnel, shattered glass, and marble chunks flying as the rounds tore through the bank.

Even so, it was immediately clear that Lucky's bodyguards—expert mercenaries—were outmanned and outgunned.

One of them was shot, and as he fell to the ground, he managed to turn and shout at Lucky, "Go!"

But Lucky shook her head.

Instead, she set her dog down inside the hallway.

"Sit!" The dog complied. "Stay!"

She shut the oak door and turned toward the bank manager, shoving him to the ground and straddling his chest with her feet spread. Then, with him cowering beneath her, she unloaded her weapon in a furious onslaught of gunfire aimed at the advancing cartel hitmen. Her first volley took out the closest gunman and wounded the man behind him.

A few seconds later, one of the hitmen gave a primordial shout and leaped across his fallen comrades in a beeline for Lucky, darting in an evasive zigzag pattern. Lucky tried to stop him, but he was growing alarmingly close and his bullets were striking the wall next to her. Then Lucky's bullets ran out. Along with her luck.

Lucky's wounded bodyguard was only a few feet in front of her on the ground. When he heard the hollow click of her trigger, he roared and leaped up from the floor. He turned and fired, taking the advancing hitman down. But his already wounded body also absorbed the rain of bullets the charging gunman had aimed at Lucky.

Both the hitman and her bodyguard sank to the ground. Neither moved again.

Furious, Lucky reached to take the AK-47 out of her dead bodyguard's hands and squeezed off a volley of shots until she emptied the weapon. Her blitz caused the remaining hitmen to take cover.

Lucky took advantage of the lull to quickly scan the room. From what she could see, the two cops were out of the gunfight—either wounded or dead—and only two of the cartel hitmen were still in play, tucked behind large marble pillars.

She saw the tip of a rifle sticking out from one pillar and, across the lobby, spotted a man's shoe sticking out from another.

Knowing the quiet moment was short-lived, Lucky stepped behind a pillar and quickly reloaded her weapon. She was pinned down, and she knew it. She focused on preparing for the inevitable attack headed her way, taking several deep breaths to center herself and imagining the exact moves she would make to go after the remaining hitmen.

If she stayed where she was, she'd be dead. She had to somehow make it to the neighboring pillar without getting shot. In her mind's eye, she visualized herself running and doing an evasive gymnastic flip to avoid the bullets aimed her way.

Nearly too late, she noticed that the remaining two hitmen had already begun their sneak attack, using military hand signals as they quickly ran to the next set of columns. Now, nothing stood between Lucky's pillar and the men. Ducking back to her cover for a second, Lucky prepared herself for her kamikaze attack.

Just as she launched herself out from behind the pillar, two quick gunshots rang out.

Already in motion, Lucky dropped into a smooth combat roll before she popped up with her finger on the trigger of her automatic rifle.

Swearing, she immediately lowered her weapon when she saw who was in her sights.

Adam Shepherd.

He stood there with his gun held loosely at his side, an infuriating smirk on his face, and two cartel hitmen dead at his feet.

"What in the hell are you doing here?" Lucky asked, her voice filled with rage.

"I was about to ask you the same thing."

8

_____

"Policia! Policia!"

Lucky and Shepherd both slanted their eyes toward the front of the bank.

They were surrounded.

Dozens of men in camouflage were pouring out of a caravan of SWAT-type armored trucks that had pulled up and overtaken the street out front.

Commands in Spanish were being shouted through a megaphone, ordering Lucky and Shepherd to surrender.

They ignored the commands.

The bank manager stood unsteadily. He straightened his tie and smoothed his hands down his pant legs, trying to regain some semblance of dignity but obviously unaware that a thick hunk of shellacked hair had flopped to one side of his head and was sticking up comically.

"I told you this was the safest bank in all of Mexico," he said in a haughty voice.

"I wouldn't be so certain of that. They're outside and we're still in here where the money is," Lucky said coolly. "If you drop that smug look off your face and cooperate, you might just live to kiss your wife, Julia, goodnight."

Julia and Lucky had enjoyed a great conversation at the cocktail party last night.

"Move your fat ass," she said.

The shouting through the megaphone continued.

"If you surrender now, you will get out alive."

Ignoring the authorities outside, Shepherd leaned down and scooped up an assault rifle and backpack from one of the dead men. He peered inside. It was filled with ammo. He slung it over his shoulder and turned to Lucky.

"Let's go."

She gave him an exasperated look but didn't say anything.

"Just so you know," he said, "we're not going out the front door."

"Thanks for the tip," Lucky said drily. "Anything else you want to add while you're taking on the role of Master of the Obvious?"

Looking sheepish, he answered, "Just hoping there's a plan to get out of here. I don't know if I can save your ass this time."

Lucky glared at him. "This time? If I remember correctly, the last time I saw you I was saving your ass."

"I'm not so sure about that," he said.

She huffed loudly.

"Besides, this is my plan. This is my job. You're not even supposed to be here, so why don't you keep your keen observations to yourself and kick it in gear."

Despite her caustic tone, Shepherd grinned at her.

"Oh, I'm supposed to be here all right."

"What are you talking about?" she said as they started back toward the oak door leading to the back hallway.

Shepherd didn't answer.

Lucky prodded the bank manager to walk in front of her.

Pushing the door open, they were greeted by Lucky's dog, who had been sitting patiently but began to wriggle madly when he saw his owner.

"Good boy," Lucky said.

"What the hell is that?" Shepherd said.

"My dog."

Eyeing Shepherd's backpack, she said, "Turn around."

"Heh?"

Lucky scooped up the dog. "He's little. He'll fit in your backpack. Safest place for him now."

Shepherd rolled his eyes but turned and let Lucky stuff the dog in the backpack as they walked. The dog's head stuck out of the unzipped top, and she leaned over and kissed its nose before patting Shepherd's shoulder. "Good to go!"

They kept walking down the hallway to where it dead-ended. To the right was a large vault. Across the hall was a steel door.

The manager stopped in front of the vault.

"Open it up," Lucky said.

"They'll be here any—"

His words faded as a loud announcement made over the PA ordered Lucky and Shepherd to surrender.

"In any case," the manager said, trying to regain a shred of his dignity, "there is no way they are letting you out of here alive."

"We'll see about that," she said. "Open it!"

The bank manager folded his arms across his chest, so Lucky stepped down hard on his shins.

"Okay, okay." He winced in pain, taking a step toward the large vault door.

Lucky shook her head.

"Not the main vault," she said. "This one."

She pointed her machine gun at the steel door with a high-tech access panel.

The manager's face grew pale. "I don't know what you are talking about."

"Cut the bullshit," Lucky said.

"We can't touch that money."

"The hell we can't."

The bank manager swallowed hard. "You don't understand. You don't know who this money belongs to."

"Actually, I do." Lucky grinned. "That's exactly why I'm here."

"I'm a dead man if I let you in there."

"You're a dead man if you don't," Shepherd said.

"This can be easy or hard. Your choice. All I need is the key around your neck." Lucky flicked it with the barrel of the machine gun. "And that eyeball in your head."

She held her machine gun a few centimeters from his eyeball. He was shaking now.

"The lock mechanism doesn't care if the eyeball is still in your head or not. And neither do I," she said. "Last chance. Open it and you live."

The manager's hand shook as he lifted the key toward the lock.

Lucky tapped the muzzle against the side of his head with a solid thwack. "This isn't my first rodeo, cowboy. I know what happens if you don't do the sequence— if you key the lock before the retinal scan."

Her gaze lifted to a recessed steel cage in the ceiling. She jutted her chin upward.

"If that cage drops, so do you."

Meanwhile, Shepherd, whose back was to them, said over his shoulder, "Looks like we've got some party crashers."

"Roger that," she said.

Shepherd continued, "If you've got an exit plan, now would be a great time to pull that baby out."

Lucky pushed the manager's head down to the retinal scan. When the light turned green, she yanked him up by the collar and held the gun to the back of his head.

They could hear shouting from the door leading to the lobby.

"Now!" Lucky screamed at the manager.

He put the key in the lock and glanced nervously up at the ceiling. The cage remained in place and the door slid open.

There was a large explosion, and the door splintered behind them.

Shepherd laid down a line of cover fire as Lucky and the manager entered the room. Shepherd ducked into the room behind them right before shots peppered the wall where they had been standing.

9

Lucky used the gun's muzzle to push the manager deeper inside the long, rectangular room. The walls were lined with lockers and safe deposit boxes. On the opposite end was a steel door that said "Utility" in Spanish.

Without hesitation, Lucky headed toward a locker in the far corner of the room.

"This one," she said. "Open it."

Sweat dripped from the manager's temples. "I don't have a key. I swear. It's kept in my office for extra security. For situations like this one."

Lucky stared at him for a long second, and for the first time that day, she faltered. She knew the manager was telling the truth.

After a few seconds of contemplation, Lucky nodded and pushed him toward Shepherd. Reaching into her bag, she extracted some det cord, and within seconds, she rigged up a makeshift explosive device.

Shepherd watched her work, and when she was done, he gave a low whistle.

"Not bad," he said. "You're even better than I remember."

Lucky stood back and pushed the button.

A small explosion blew off the locker door, revealing thick stacks of bills wrapped in cellophane.

Lucky reached into her tote and pulled out a folded duffle bag. Crouching, she began to load the money inside.

The manager mopped at his brow. "You can't touch that money. You take that, I'm a dead man. Take anything but that money. That's Orozco's money. The second you walk out the door with that money—even if you're lucky enough to get past the cartel hit squad—you're a dead woman."

At the word "lucky," she and Shepherd exchanged a smirk.

The bank manager caught it and shook his head.

"You both are crazy. Insane. And you're both dead. Guaranteed. You have no idea what you have done."

"The only person who's going to be dead is you if you don't shut up," Lucky said.

With the duffle bag strap looped over her shoulder, she nodded at Shepherd.

Shouts and banging came from the hallway.

Shepherd put his ear to the door.

"We've got company," he said. "Sounds like a SWAT team. They're getting ready to breach this door. It's going to blow any second."

Shepherd faced the door with his AK-47 at the ready.

Lucky turned to the manager. "Take us out the secure door."

"I don't know what you mean."

Lucky gave an exasperated sigh and flicked open the latch on the metal door labeled "Utility." Behind it was a thick door with a high-tech lock.

"When they come in shooting, they aren't going to miss, and they aren't going to miss you either."

Without a word, the manager leaned over, pressed his face to the retinal scan, and inserted the key. With a loud hiss, the door slid open, revealing a narrow hallway with an elevator at the far end.

They stepped inside and slammed the door shut just as the vault door was breached in a hail of gunfire and shouting. The three raced to the elevator and stepped inside, Lucky punching the down button.

The elevator door opened into a long tunnel that led under the bank, ending at a short flight of stairs. Pushing the manager in front of them, Lucky and Shepherd raced up the stairs and opened the door at the top.

They entered a small shop selling tarot cards, oils, and incense before rushing through another door, finding themselves inside the kitchen of the café across the street. From there, they hustled out to the dining room.

Lucky had her assault rifle pointed at the bank manager, prodding him through the dining room. Several people screamed and drew back. Shepherd, bringing up the rear, was smiling and saying, "Excuse us. Coming through. Pardon me."

When they got to the front door, Lucky shoved the bank manager over to a nearby table.

"Sit your ass down and count to ten before you leave."

As Lucky and Shepherd stepped into the sunlight, the manager yelled at them, "You're both dead, you know?"

Shepherd looked at Lucky and smirked.

"We've heard that before."

10

Shepherd and Lucky both blinked as they stepped out into the bright sunlight.

The street held the aftermath of a massacre. Four dead bodies were splayed on the road, including her driver.

A group of police officers and SWAT team members milled about on the bank's front steps.

Lucky and Shepherd walked quickly toward an alley on their side of the street. They'd almost made it when one of the officers spotted them.

"There they are!"

Police rushed across the street toward them, guns raised, yelling, "Freeze!"

Lucky had just rounded the corner, Shepherd at her heels, when a black truck squealed to a stop between them and the other end of the alley.

Cartel hitmen.

Shepherd and Lucky split up and simultaneously dove for cover behind parked cars right before a man in the back of the truck began to fire a .50cal machine gun mounted to the center of the truck bed. The onslaught from the cartel hitmen stopped the onrush of federal police, forcing them to retreat.

Crouched behind vehicles on opposite sides of the alley, Lucky and

Shepherd exchanged a look. Shepherd held up three fingers, and when Lucky nodded, he started the countdown.

When the last finger dropped, Shepherd stood and, with a terrific shout, began to fire methodically. His first shots took out the two cartel hitmen flanking the machine gun, leaving one man on the truck bed. At the same time, Lucky darted forward, firing her own machine gun and taking out the driver of the truck before she dove into an alcove.

A few seconds later, she darted out again, firing at the truck as she approached it. The machine gun swiveled to track her, but its trajectory could only move 180 degrees on its mount so it stopped before it was pointed at Lucky. With the last remaining hitman's attention on Lucky's advance, Shepherd raced to the other side of the truck and took him out with a single shot to the back of the head.

As soon as the man slumped to the truck bed, the federal police moved in, using a bearcat as cover. One officer roared into a megaphone in Spanish as the bearcat grew closer.

"Surrender! Hands up! You are surrounded and under arrest."

Shepherd didn't lower his weapon or fire. Without moving, he scanned the alley.

They weren't actually surrounded.

Now that they'd taken out the armored cartel truck, their path to the other end of the alley—and freedom—was clear.

"Go!" he shouted to Lucky. "I'll hold them."

She paused, raising an eyebrow, and he bellowed even louder, "Run!"

Shepherd laid down a suppressive round of gunfire in front of the approaching police officers, clearly shooting to impede them, not hit them.

Seeing this, the police officer in charge shouted for his team to hold their fire, but too late: a bullet struck Shepherd's left shoulder. Recoiling, Shepherd stumbled and fell backward. He caught himself with his other arm, but before he could scramble to his feet, the Pomeranian managed to wriggle out of the open backpack and run.

Taking cover behind the truck bed, Shepherd examined his shoulder. The bullet had just grazed him.

Lucky, nearing the end of the alley, paused when she saw Shepherd was shot.

He turned, met her eyes, and mouthed, "Go!"

Nodding, Lucky turned back to run and then froze.

Her dog was barking furiously and charging the police officers.

A few turned and pointed their guns at it.

"No!" she shouted.

"Don't shoot!" Shepherd yelled. "Leave the dog alone! I surrender!"

He stepped out from behind the truck and held his hands in the air.

Then he turned and put his hands over his head, giving Lucky a last look as police officers swarmed him.

Given no choice, Lucky turned and ran.

He breathed a long sigh of relief when he saw that both she and the dog managed to get away, then braced himself as the Federal Mexican Police tactical officers reached him and threw him to the ground. He didn't fight back. They pummeled him with their batons and kicked him with their steel-toe boots, berating him and swearing at him.

He covered his head with his forearms and tried to tighten his abdominal muscles to hopefully avoid a set of broken ribs or worse.

As suddenly as the beatings started, they stopped. A senior officer was shouting at the men, scolding them. He ordered them to cuff Shepherd and stuff him in the back of a nearby squad car.

Once seated, Shepherd had a chance to look around. The dog was gone. Good.

11

Lucky stripped off the leather blazer, and the silky pants puddled on the floor as she stepped into the tiny but clean hotel room shower.

She'd been waiting ten minutes for the water to get hot until she realized it would never happen. Now, she steeled herself for the shock of the icy pellets raining down on her bare flesh.

Telling herself it was good for her, shocking her mitochondria cells into regenerating themselves, she still gasped as she stepped into the shower.

For the first time, she had to admit that while the ostentatious house in Campestre was not her style, she'd actually enjoyed the small luxuries— the fully stocked refrigerator, down-filled bed, and mostly, the consistent hot showers.

But that house would be the first place the bank manager would send the police to look for her. She'd cleaned it out thoroughly, even making sure to wipe down any surface that might have captured a fingerprint.

Now, as she stood shivering under the freezing water, she tried to convince herself it was invigorating. She lathered up the rough, grainy soap and scrubbed her flesh until it was bright red. Every cell in her body wanted to get out of the shower and climb under the bedcovers, but she forced herself to stay until the dial on her watch hit the twelve. Ten more minutes.

She'd grown soft. It was time to get back in the game. This motel with cold water was a virtual palace compared to places during past ops.

Thinking of those ops made her shake her head.

She pushed back memories of the horrors of war-torn countries where terror reigned and bloodied body parts were scattered across the rubble of collapsed buildings amid the heart-wrenching sounds of a small child weeping.

As the cold water pelted down on her back, Lucky leaned against the shower wall and absentmindedly reached for the tiny gold horn pendant on its delicate gold chain. It was all she had left of her father, a cheap bauble compared to the other jewelry she owned, but priceless in her eyes.

It was a smaller version of the pendant her Italian mother had always worn. Sofia Toscani was buried in that necklace the year Lucky was twelve.

In Italian culture, the cornicello horn, which protected you from the evil eye, couldn't be bought. It had to be a gift. Her Mexican father had saved his money as a farmer and bought the gold-plated necklace for her sixteenth birthday.

She hadn't taken it off since.

Then her thoughts turned to the day's events.

Seeing Shepherd had thrown her off her game.

It was both odd and normal.

A long time ago, she'd thought he always would be there with her.

Until he wasn't.

That was why she'd been so stunned to see him in the bank lobby.

She'd gotten used to his absence. How dare he come back around?

Stepping out of the shower, she squeezed all the water from her hair, yanking it back so tightly it hurt.

Despite her best efforts to be free of him, he was back.

She should've known that he would pop back into her life when she least expected.

Angrily, she dried herself off with the rough motel towel, enjoying the way it scraped her soft skin. Despite her face being hot with anger, her body quaked with cold.

Shepherd.

He'd screwed everything up this time.

If he hadn't butted in, she'd have been fine. Better than fine. Fantastic. She didn't need him. She'd never needed him.

Standing naked before the mirror, she held the hair dryer to her long, dark hair, not meeting her own eyes in the reflection because a small part of her knew she was lying.

The bank heist had gone sideways, and without Shepherd's help, she might easily be the one behind bars in a Mexican holding cell.

The big lunk had sacrificed for her. And her dog.

Damn it all.

Now there was no way she'd leave Mexico without getting him out of jail first.

Then, hopefully, she would never see him again.

Once again, she was lying to herself.

12

La Perejila was one of the few restaurants that not only survived the bloody decade of cartel war but thrived during it.

Red-velvet wallpaper lined the dining area, black marble coated the floors, and the low ceilings were covered in dark beams. Everything was old-school plush and rich-looking, from the black velvet-tufted dining chairs, to the gilt-framed mirrors that reflected the flickering candlelight, to the sparkling crystal cut glasses and glittering chandeliers.

All the cartel leaders had declared the five-star treasure off limits during their war.

They'd decided they wanted a place to impress their simpering mistresses, appease their haughty wives, and celebrate their daughters' quinceañeras.

The one time a cartel hitman had violated this treaty and fired at a rival cartel member exiting the restaurant, an example had been made of him.

His head had been cut off and stuck on a wall opposite the restaurant as a warning to those who dared violate this simple request.

Now that the violence in Juarez had simmered down slightly, Victor Orozco Jr. treated the restaurant like his own personal kitchen.

Like his infamous father, Orozco was a small but compact man who commanded authority. He was only five foot four and 165 pounds, carrying all his weight in his large chest and stomach. Unlike his father, who had a receding hairline at thirty, Orozco Jr.'s full head of wavy black hair and bushy black mustache were still going strong at forty-five.

However, he had his father's long aquiline nose and didn't hesitate to look down it at those who served him. Like the owner of La Perejila, for instance.

When the cartel leader came in, the owner knew if he wanted the cartel's continued protection, he needed to make Orozco feel like a king.

Even tonight, as the mayor of Juarez grew annoyed at his own table, the owner ignored him to dote on Orozco, his wife Fernanda, and Dominguez, his head of security.

And that meant offering their table a bottle of the finest wine.

"This bottle, of course, is not on the menu," the owner said, proffering it for their inspection. A thin sheen of perspiration glistened above the man's thin upper lip. He reminded Orozco of a weasel with his long nose and close-set beady eyes.

Orozco was confused that he found the man's obsequious manner both flattering and annoying. But, alas, sacrifices had to be made. Right now, he was only concerned with pleasing his wife.

"My dear?" he asked. "Are you feeling in the mood for red tonight?"

Instead of answering, Fernanda flicked her startling green eyes to Dominguez. The head of security carefully scrutinized the label, his eyebrows furrowed. Then he reached for his phone. Seconds later, he held it out to Fernanda and then Orozco.

The bottle was worth three thousand dollars.

"That will do," Fernanda said.

The woman liked expensive things, that was certain.

Her hobby was spending his money. But while she was certainly a handsome woman, she was no trophy wife. She was his closest confidante. Without her by his side, he would not have risen to the level he had in life. He conveniently forgot that he had simply inherited his role as cartel leader when his father died two years ago.

Through all those years of having to put up with his father's condescending bullshit, Fernanda had been there to cool his hot head. When he'd wanted to rebel and lash out against his father, she'd been the one to remind him that the man was old and ill.

When he'd wanted to start his own business, she'd reminded him to be patient.

"All of this will be yours before you are fifty," she'd told him. "Patience."

And she'd been right. He'd been forty-one when his father had suffered a massive stroke and died in his sleep. Thanks to Fernanda, everything had already been arranged for him to seamlessly step into his father's shoes.

When Orozco remembered how smoothly it had gone, he blocked out the many times he'd come upon his father and Fernanda having a late nightcap in the palatial family home, laughing with their heads close together.

The first time he'd expressed jealousy, Fernanda's green eyes had blazed. "Do you want to be the master of your destiny or just a little boy scuttling about under his father's footsteps? If you want to be king of Mexico, do not interfere with what I do and say."

He'd been suitably chastised. But from then on, he'd grown to hate his father. When the doctor had expressed concerns about his father's death, Orozco had arranged to have him killed. On Fernanda's advice, of course.

His only regret was that he and his wife had never had children.

She'd told him she was unable to bear children and he'd believed her, even when he found evidence that she had an IUD inside her.

None of that mattered.

Everything they'd worked for had come to fruition.

Soon, he would be the most powerful man in Mexico.

Only a few more puzzle pieces remained to be put in place.

Now, Orozco glanced around the restaurant, pleased to see the other diners shooting looks his way. Looks of admiration, he surmised.

This was the most expensive restaurant in all of Juarez, full of women in fur coats and dripping diamonds, and yet the manager dropped everything if Orozco even raised an eyebrow.

Located on the fanciest street in Juarez's most exclusive neighborhood, it was the place to be seen. Reservations had to be made a month in advance. At least.

Even so, if Victor Orozco walked in and wanted his regular table, a reservation meant nothing. Not even if you were the president of Mexico himself.

This restaurant was a microcosm of his rule.

He haughtily sniffed the small amount of wine the owner had poured in his glass and then took a sip. He gave a dismissive wave of his hand. "It is fine."

As the owner walked away, Dominguez, who had his lanky back to the wall, now leaned down to fill Orozco in on the astonishing events of the day.

The gray-haired Dominguez absentmindedly scratched one long sideburn as he spoke, his mouth down by Orozco's ear, his eyes still relentlessly scanning the restaurant for any possible threats despite the treaty.

As Dominguez explained that Guzman had pulled out of their deal, ending with the news that Orozco's cash had been taken during a bank robbery—by a woman, no less—Orozco's face grew red.

The cartel leader attempted to stand and head toward the kitchen, but Dominguez had placed a hand on his boss's Armani-clad shoulder and spoke a reassuring word in his ear, so Orozco settled back down.

"Who was she?" he asked.

Dominguez shrugged. "The big guy isn't talking. That will change. He'll squeal, we'll find the *puta*, and we'll get our money back."

"That's eight hundred thousand dollars in twenty-four hours," Orozco snarled beneath his thick black mustache.

Across the table, Fernanda, who was watching the two men with her piercing eyes, set down her wine glass hard enough to shake the table.

Both men stopped speaking and looked up.

Once again, Orozco looked at his wife in admiration. She was thin as a bird but had a full bosom thanks to surgery. Her green eyes were stunning against her bronze skin and sheet of silky black hair. Her hooked nose combined with her impeccable posture and bearing made her appear regal. He had always been proud to have such an attractive, shrewd woman at his side.

"A woman?" she said, and sneered. "You were robbed by a woman?"

Then she burst into laughter.

"Dominguez is mistaken," Orozco said. "This woman was the sidekick for a very dangerous man. She is nothing. We have him and that's what counts."

He quickly nodded at the owner, who rushed over to refill their wine glasses.

As soon as he did, Orozco raised his glass and turned to Dominguez. "We will talk about business later. Tonight, I want to enjoy the company of my lovely wife."

Dominguez nodded stiffly.

While they spoke, an older couple had entered the restaurant, and as the maître d' led them past Orozco's table, the man stopped and bowed.

"Please forgive me," the man said. "May I please have just a small moment of your time?"

Orozco gave an indulgent nod.

"Thank you, Mr. Orozco," the man said. "I owe you for my wife's life. Without the hospital you built, my wife would surely have died. Please allow me to pay for your meal tonight."

Basking in the feeling of ruling over his small fiefdom, Orozco puffed out his chest and reached over to pat the man's wrinkled and age-spotted hand.

"Your kind words are payment enough," he said.

Behind the man, the wrinkled wife, who was wearing a scarf to cover her balding head from cancer treatments, teared up.

"In fact, you would do me a great honor," Orozco said, "if you allow me to pay for your dinner tonight instead."

The man dropped to his creaky knees and kissed Orozco's hand, muttering praises in rapid-fire Spanish.

Orozco allowed the man to do so for a good two minutes before he said, "Go now and enjoy your dinner."

Giving the rest of the diners a benevolent gaze, Orozco turned to the owner and said, "Be sure to take care of them. Bring up a second bottle. They have something worth celebrating."

All heads were still turned toward Orozco so he raised his voice and his glass.

"Please join me in this toast," he said, "to a long life worth living."

The restaurant erupted into cheers. The older man rose from his knees with tears in his eyes as the maître d' led the couple to their table.

Orozco turned to Dominguez. "You see, my friend, this is the true power I wield. This is the future. And we will be the ones to make this a reality for all."

Dominguez offered a silent nod, his craggy, lined face expressionless.

Orozco leaned over to his wife and spoke just above a whisper, but intentionally loud enough for Dominguez to hear.

"Our good friend Dominguez here doesn't think that this is how we should conduct ourselves. He would prefer these glasses be filled with the blood of our enemies."

Dominguez remained expressionless.

Fernanda didn't respond except to raise one perfectly shaped eyebrow.

Orozco continued. "But we are on the cusp of a future that will change everything. No more fighting for table scraps. No more acting like street criminals and thugs." He unfolded his cloth napkin and set it on his lap. "Soon, very soon, we will no longer be bound by border walls. We will no longer be prisoners. We will rise to power in a way my father could never have envisioned."

Fernanda's mouth spread into a Mona Lisa smile. She lifted her glass, but before it met her crimson lips, she froze, hand and glass in mid-air as the restaurant door was flung open.

A woman with sunglasses and a long, dark ponytail strode through the door. She wore combat boots below black cargo pants and a chic leather bomber jacket.

All conversation and sound in the restaurant came to a grinding halt as the woman loped through the restaurant straight toward Orozco's table.

Fernanda sneered at the approaching woman.

"What is she doing here?" she said.

Dominguez was reaching for his gun when Orozco held up a hand. "Wait," he said. He gave his wife a questioning glance.

The woman was lugging an obviously heavy black duffle bag.

Heads turned as everyone watched her walk through the restaurant.

As soon as she reached Orozco's table, she dropped the bag onto the white tablecloth with a thud.

13

Behind her oversized dark sunglasses, Lucky watched Orozco's eyes narrow as he looked up from the duffle bag.

He knew what was in the bag. He knew who she was.

Or at least he knew what she was—a bank robber.

Standing in front of his table with one hip cocked out and her hand on her waist, she sighed as if she were impatient with waiting. Her head didn't move, but she clocked the bodyguard standing against the wall near the table. He wore a faded beige button-down top and brown slacks. His thick black hair was shot with gray and his eyes were cold underneath gray-streaked eyebrows.

He had an engraved pistol in a holster on his right side, another weapon stuffed in his back waistband, and probably a serious knife or two strapped to his ankle.

The bodyguard kept his eyes trained on her.

Lucky immediately knew who he was: the Orozco Cartel's deadliest killer. Despite his relaxed attitude, Lucky didn't underestimate the man for one second. He was a death dealer of the highest caliber.

On the opposite side of the table was that dried-up witch, Fernanda Orozco.

Lucky had made sure to avoid any direct contact with the woman at last night's cocktail party.

It had only taken one glance at Fernanda to know that the older woman was shrewd and would see right through Lucky's prima donna act.

Even so, the two had a brief encounter in the bathroom right before Lucky left.

Fernanda had followed her inside, and then, instead of using the stall, she stood in front of the mirror until Lucky came out.

With her thin, Armani-clad hip resting on the edge of the sink, Fernanda had said, "You have an interesting accent. Or, rather, you don't have an accent at all."

"Really?" Lucky's voice was cool, unruffled.

"Where did you say you are from again?"

"I didn't," Lucky said, and walked out.

After that, Lucky had decided it was time to leave. Even though she didn't know all the details, the woman had sniffed her out.

Better to leave before she started asking questions and making comments to other party guests. Particularly, the former assistant bank manager, who had been drunk and extremely forthcoming with details about the bank and its security when Lucky had expressed doubt that her money would be safe there. The woman had scoffed and said anyone could get to the vault if they held a gun to the manager's head.

It had been solid intel, and was one reason Lucky now had a duffle bag full of the cartel leader's cash.

Now, looking over at Orozco's wife, Lucky knew she'd been recognized the instant she opened the restaurant door.

After a few seconds of silence, Orozco spoke to Dominguez.

"Please remove this bag so my guest may have room to sit with us at our table."

The bodyguard scooped the bag up from the table by its handles.

The vein in Orozco's neck throbbed and his teeth were clenched. Lucky saw that he was barely able to control the rage bubbling inside him at her insolence. Like a scientist examining a specimen, she watched, fascinated, wondering what would happen next.

While Dominguez was a stone-cold killer, Lucky also was armed with two guns and a knife. Going head to head with the notorious bodyguard was a dangerous prospect, but Lucky had one small advantage—the element of surprise.

The cocky old cowboy would never believe a woman like her could be a real threat. Being underestimated had always been one of her secret weapons.

As Lucky watched, Fernanda reached for Orozco's hand. The touch seemed to calm the drug lord enough to allow him to give in to his curiosity. His eyes freely roamed over Lucky's body, beginning at her feet and traveling slowly upward.

She didn't flinch, glad that the dark sunglasses hid the daggers shooting from her eyes.

"I don't know what kind of game you're playing," he said finally.

"It's not a game. It's an audition." Lucky tossed her head toward Dominguez, still holding the duffle bag. "Consider that my resume. I'm applying for a job."

Orozco stood. The other diners once again grew quiet.

With a tight smile, Orozco reached over, plucked a chair from a nearby table, and put it next to his. He gestured at it, looking at Lucky.

She ignored him and remained standing.

Seeming unflustered, he sat down and took a sip of his wine before looking back up at Lucky.

"Stealing from me is not the way to gain my trust."

"The manager at your bank assured me that it was the safest bank in Mexico—just moments before I walked away with all your money," Lucky responded.

"Are you saying that stealing from me is easy?"

Lucky jutted her chin toward the duffle bag and smirked, her red lips curling.

Orozco frowned.

Ignoring the chair he'd placed for her, Lucky reached behind her and grabbed a chair from a different table, placing it next to Fernanda, who winced and scooted away.

"Who are you?" Orozco asked, finally giving in to his curiosity.

"Don't you remember me?" Lucky asked. When he looked confused, she took off her sunglasses and placed them on the table. Then she yanked her long hair out of its ponytail and shook it so it fell loosely across her shoulders. "Let me refresh your memory."

Orozco's eyes widened as recognition dawned.

"Victor, she was at the cocktail party last night." Fernanda rolled her eyes, reaching for her wine glass. "Her name is Eve or something. You probably don't recognize her face because you were too busy staring at her tits and ass."

Orozco's mouth opened in shock. "You?"

"*El gusto es mio*," she said, and stuck out her hand. "I'm Evelyn Rodriguez-Toscani. My friends call me Lucky."

Orozco shot Dominguez a look. The other man took out a cell phone and began typing.

"Are you?" Orozco asked. "Lucky?"

Lucky met his gaze. "Depends on who you ask."

Unconsciously, she reached up and stroked the necklace her father had given her. He'd been the one to nickname her Lucky after a series of coincidences had spared her life.

The first time, she'd been two years old and survived a terrible car crash with family members who were watching her while her mother worked. She had been thrown from the car and miraculously landed on a large creosote bush in full bloom. When the authorities found her, she smelled like flowers after a hard rain.

A few years later, she'd been at a friend's house when cartel hitmen showed up. They stormed inside and shot everyone they saw. Everybody died except Lucky. She'd been on the floor near a table leg. In the chaos, a pitcher of water had been knocked off the table and struck her temple. The blow had knocked her out and the hitmen left, thinking she was dead.

The third instance had involved her and some classmates playing in an abandoned building that caught on fire. Her two friends had been trapped inside and burned to death.

All the parents had rushed to the charred building, wailing and crying. Lucky shocked them all by walking around the side of the building barefoot, her face smeared with soot.

Right before the explosion, she'd heard someone crying out back and went to investigate. A few seconds later, a small explosion rocked the building and it went up in flames.

She'd been five years old.

That's when her dad started calling her Lucky.

"What's your real name?" Fernanda asked.

The question startled Lucky out of her reverie. Fernanda's eyes narrowed as she watched Lucky touch the necklace.

"I told you," Lucky said.

Dominguez approached Orozco and leaned over, showing his phone screen.

"What? What is it?" Fernanda said.

Orozco pointed the phone toward Fernanda. Lucky recognized the picture he held up, a Texas Rangers wanted poster with her picture and a detailed description.

"So," Orozco said, "you're good at bank robberies—quite a few of them, it appears—but are you good at stealing from other places?"

"I guess you'll have to find out," Lucky said.

Orozco bit his lip and looked at her as if trying to see right through her.

"I have had problems with my security in the past." He cut a sharp look at Dominguez, who nearly imperceptibly winced. "And you've obviously pointed out a weakness I must address."

Orozco paused and sat back in his chair. "But the fact remains that you stole from me. What kind of message am I sending if I allow someone to do that and remain unpunished?"

"Especially if it was a woman, right?" Lucky said.

Orozco frowned.

Lucky leaned forward and put her palms on the table. "I didn't actually steal from you." She nodded at the duffle bag. "I merely borrowed it for a few hours. It's all there. I never intended to keep it."

She locked eyes with Orozco. Finally, he smiled.

The waiter arrived and refilled Orozco's and Fernanda's wine glasses.

"Wait," Orozco said. "Please bring a glass for our guest."

Then he turned to Lucky. "When someone borrows money from me, I always charge interest."

The waiter reappeared and poured a glass of wine for Lucky.

She lifted the glass toward Orozco, paused, then took a drink. She took her time setting the glass back down.

Then, very deliberately, she slid a massive diamond ring off her finger and placed it on the white tablecloth in front of Orozco.

Without looking at it, Orozco nodded at Dominguez, who picked up the ring and handed it to Fernanda.

The older woman placed it in her palm and eyed it, shrugging.

"It's okay," she said.

"It's worth thirteen thousand dollars," Lucky said flatly, not taking her eyes off Orozco.

Fernanda shrugged again.

"Okay," she said.

Lucky was about to sit back in her chair when Fernanda continued speaking. "The ring." She paused. "And your necklace."

"What?" Lucky said, taken off guard.

"The ring and the necklace."

Lucky's jaw tightened but she smiled. "Of course."

She unclasped the necklace and laid it on the table.

Orozco scoffed. "That ugly, cheap thing? Really, Fernanda?"

"Yes," his wife said.

"Very well, then." Orozco gave Fernanda an indulgent smile. "The key to a happy marriage is to give the woman everything she asks for."

"But of course," Lucky said in a calm voice, her eyes flashing dangerously.

Fernanda swept the necklace off the table into her palm.

After a few minutes of silence, Orozco nodded. "I must say this is the most unique job interview I've ever had the pleasure of giving. I think I just might have an opportunity for you to prove your worth."

"Really?" Lucky said coolly.

"Have you heard of Alejandro Guzman?"

"But of course," Lucky said. "Owns Desire Nightclub outside of Nogales."

Orozco beamed. "Very good."

"I made sure I knew who your competitors were before I applied for this position."

"Competitors?" Orozco's face reddened. "Guzman is no competition."

"The phrasing was unfortunate," Lucky said. "I should have said that I made a point to unearth the pesky mosquitos that have been bothersome to you over the years."

Orozco broke into laughter. "Exactly," he said. "This particular mosquito, let's call him, owes me money. He keeps it in a safe room in the club behind his personal lounge."

"If you know where he keeps his money, why don't you just go take it?" Lucky said, and took another sip of her wine.

Orozco sighed. "Normally I would, but this situation is a bit complicated and delicate, I would call it. I need you to get the money. As soon as possible."

Lucky stood. "What's my cut?"

Dominguez reached for his gun. Orozco didn't stop him this time. Instead, he burst into laughter at Lucky's words.

"You have some *cajones* on you, I'll give you that," he said.

"I'm serious." Lucky's eyes narrowed.

"Your cut?" Orozco's voice grew hard for the first time. "Your cut is I don't cut your throat and drain your blood into a wine glass for Dominguez here to drink."

Lucky tensed. Her fingers, resting at her side, itched to reach for the gun she had tucked in her back waistband under her leather jacket.

A flush had risen from Orozco's neck to his jowls. Fernanda reached over and patted his hand. He inhaled sharply and then slowly exhaled.

Lucky instantly relaxed.

"Dominguez will be in touch. He will arrange everything." Orozco reached for his wine glass and drained it.

Lucky didn't move.

When he set it back down, he seemed surprised that she was still standing there.

"I'll get your money," she said. "I just need one thing."

"Yes?" he asked. "I'm feeling indulgent. Maybe it's the wine." He chuckled.

"I need my friend. The one who was arrested for the bank robbery."

"What?" Orozco laughed. "That's the one thing you need? I said I was feeling indulgent. I never said I was Saint Nicholas."

He turned toward Dominguez. "And here I thought she was going to ask for an AR-15."

Lucky still hadn't moved.

"What you want me to do, I can only do with my friend's help. We're a team."

Orozco squinted at Dominguez. "Isn't he dead by now?"

Dominguez shrugged. "Probably."

"I want my friend," Lucky repeated.

Dominguez scoffed. "Your friend shot at Mexican police officers. He's never getting out of that jail."

Lucky ignored him and kept her cold, dead eyes trained on Orozco.

"It's not possible," he said.

Her voice rose when she spoke next, and the diners not already glued to the conversation turned to look.

"You're telling me that Victor Orozco Jr. cannot get a lowly man out of a Mexican jail?"

The room erupted with the tinkle of her scornful laughter.

A panicked look appeared on Orozco's face. Heads turned to look at him and he balled his hands into fists as his face grew red.

He clenched his jaw and was about to respond, but Lucky had already turned on one heel and walked out of the restaurant without another word.

14

Shepherd sat hunched over in the interrogation room at the Juarez City Jail with his hands cuffed before him and his head hanging down over them.

His shirt was ripped, revealing several raised scars across his muscular back. A large cut zigzagged up the left side of his face, where it met a black and swollen eye. The bridge of his nose was also cut during the police beating and he'd ripped off a small piece of his shirt to stem the bleeding. The fabric had dried across his nose in a makeshift bandage. His lower lip was split and the blood had dried at the corner of his mouth.

He could easily see the intake processing area through the glass door separating his room from the old, worn lobby. The entire floor smelled like sweat and piss and stale vomit. The floors were smeared with the trail of a mop that had simply moved the dirt around in a swirling pattern.

As he waited, Shepherd watched a woman in a very short black dress, big hair, and red lipstick being escorted into the facility. She was not cuffed, and she walked ahead of the guards accompanying her.

As she passed, some prostitutes sitting on a bench shouted and swore at her, but she ignored them, walking with her head held high, on the way to meet some wealthy inmate who summoned her. The inmates definitely ran the asylum around here. Wealthy and powerful prisoners could order up anything from the outside—fancy food, drugs, even prostitutes.

Seconds later, Shepherd watched through the window as the red-eyed American gave him a desperate glance as he was led away into the prison interior.

When Shepherd first arrived, the kid had nearly jumped out of his seat with excitement until a guard had slammed him back down.

"Are you American? Hey, big guy! Hulk Hogan! Over here! Oh my God, are you American? I swear the drugs aren't mine. They planted them on me. I swear."

Are you American?

The question unexpectedly sent Shepherd's thoughts spiraling back to a bloody war scene.

They were both covered in children's blood when Lucky had looked at him and asked if he was American.

He'd proudly displayed the United States flag to answer her.

Her revulsion had stunned him.

Until he realized why. When he heard the whole story, he was equally revolted.

It had changed everything.

He was still proud to be American. Damn proud.

But what he had discovered that day made him hesitate anytime anyone asked him.

Seeing what his country had done to innocent children had forever changed the trajectory of his life. Seeing what a farce it had been to dedicate his entire life to the US military only to be betrayed? He would never get over it. Never.

"Sorry, kid," he'd finally said to the young man sitting in the Juarez jail. "I can't help you."

Of all the things Shepherd could've imagined happening next, he never thought the kid would begin to cry. But he had.

"You've got to get a hold of my dad. His name is Ari Levy. He's a doctor in San Francisco. Please tell him I'm here."

Then the guards had nudged Shepherd into the interrogation room and he could no longer see the kid.

Now, Shepherd turned his attention away from the lobby when the sergeant across from him gave a long sigh.

The man had spent the last thirty minutes futilely plying Shepherd with questions. Now, the sergeant slammed his notebook shut and stood, nodding to the guard outside the room to let him out.

Before the door opened, two men with assault rifles moved into place, pointing their weapons at Shepherd, who didn't even look up as the door opened and closed again.

He could hear the jail personnel talking about him on the other side of the door in Spanish.

"Give up so easily, Sarge?"

"Just taking a break," the man said.

"Did you see his back? His arms? He's got a resume of violence written all over him," one man said.

"Yeah, he's been in it. But who is he? I never saw him before."

"I can't even get him to say his name," the sergeant said.

"Just run his prints," someone said.

"He has none," the sergeant said.

"What?"

"Fingertips are filed off."

"*Dios mio!*"

"We can always run his DNA," someone said, and the room burst into laughter.

"Aren't you still waiting on the DNA from that triple murder in El Roble?"

"Yeah. Been six months."

"Give me a swig of that," the sergeant said. "I'm going back in."

"Good luck with that."

Shepherd, who could hear every word, shook his head.

The door opened again.

Back inside the room, the sergeant wagged a finger in Shepherd's face. "I'm losing my patience," he yelled in English. "I've got a job to do here and you're making it harder. You don't want to make my job harder, *pendejo*. I can make you disappear."

He snapped his fingers. "Like that."

The sergeant's face was now bright red.

Shepherd kept his head hung low, avoiding eye contact and not reacting to the yelling.

"This is your last chance to talk."

When Shepherd didn't respond, the sergeant lowered his voice.

"Fine. We know how to deal with men like you. You're not in America anymore. We do things a little differently around here. You don't want to talk? You think you're so tough? You're not tough. You have no idea what tough is. My country? We know what tough is. You Americans are like little princesses who cry if they get a bruise."

Pausing in his diatribe, the sergeant knocked on the door. The guards moved into place again as the sergeant opened the door.

"This guy thinks he's funny. He doesn't want to talk, so let's see if spending a few hours with Chavez and his crew can convince him."

An older, thin guard with a long handlebar mustache pointed an assault rifle at Shepherd. "Follow me."

When Shepherd first stood, revealing his size, the other guards with the rifles backed up. But he kept his head down and shoulders hunched as he followed the older guard and another younger man into the hall. Once they passed through another secure door that slammed behind them, the older guard led Shepherd down the hall while the younger guard took up the rear. The lighting was dim, most bulbs either burned out or flickering. The concrete walls were dotted with mold and unidentifiable stains. A musty odor combined with sweat and feces permeated the space.

As they passed various cells, the inmates began to bang on the bars and cat-call Shepherd, calling him *guapo gringo*.

The guard stopped and banged his baton on the bars of one cell. A group of men inside turned toward the door. The cell door slid open and the guard attempted to shove Shepherd inside, but it was like trying to push a brick wall. He ended up stumbling backward instead.

An inmate across the hall cackled. "A new playmate for Chavez!"

Nearly a dozen men were crowded in the cell before Shepherd.

The corner nearest the open door held a pile of feces and puddles of piss.

"It's the gringo from the bank today," one of the men inside the cell said.

Another spat on the ground. "That *esse*? He shot my man Diego."

"Get in or I shoot you in the back," the younger guard said.

Resigned, Shepherd grunted and stepped inside the cell. The door slid shut behind him. He turned and held his handcuffed wrists to the bars.

The younger guard shot him a cocky smile and shook his head.

Shepherd sighed loudly and turned to face the men in the cell.

"Chavez," the older guard said, "this gringo needs someone to teach him how things work around here."

"Let him through," a voice called from the back of the cell.

The inmates parted, revealing a man sitting at a bench in the back. He had greasy hair pulled back in a long ponytail and a handlebar mustache. He wore a blindingly white tank top that showed sinewy muscles. His arms were covered in tattoos that snaked up to his neck. A massive tattoo of Santa Muerte, the angel of death, took up his left bicep. His right arm featured a smiling devil's head. But the most prominent tattoo was the small eyeless skull right on the bridge of his nose between his eyebrows. It marked him as a cartel killer with a high body count.

The man squinted at Shepherd as he took a long drag off a cigarette. Then his face spread into a wide grin, revealing several gold teeth. "This should be fun," he said.

He nodded, and the group of men converged on Shepherd.

15

The diners at the restaurant, including Orozco, were silent as they watched Lucky stride out. As soon as the door slammed shut behind her, the tension eased and conversation resumed.

The restaurant filled with voices and the clink of silverware on porcelain as people dug back into their salmon ravioli and shrimp and lobster scampi and sipped their fine wines.

When he noticed all eyes had been on him, Orozco had barely managed to conceal his rage. Now, with that bitch gone and conversation resumed, he closed his eyes and took ten deep breaths to regain control. Across the table, Fernanda rolled her eyes at him and broke off a piece of bread, carefully spreading a miniscule slice of butter over it.

Then Orozco's eyes snapped open. His left eye was still twitching but he seemed calmer.

"Make sure her friend is dead within the hour," he said to Dominguez, who punched a number on his cell phone.

His thick mustache twitched as he said into his phone, "Where's the big guy?"

Dominguez listened, frowning.

"With Chavez?" he said.

Orozco looked up at the name and smiled.

"Make sure his body is disposed of discreetly," Dominguez said, and hung up.

Nodding at his security man, Orozco stood and kissed Fernanda on the brow.

"Give me a moment, love," he said, and walked toward the kitchen.

"Hurry," she called after him. "I'm hungry. And be sure to get a doggie bag of bones and scraps for Kiki. She'll smell us and know in an instant we went out to eat without her!"

"Of course, my love," he said, then muttered, "She loves that idiot dog more than me."

But he quickly plastered a smile on his face. It was show time.

As he made his way back to the kitchen, he stopped to smile, shake hands, and exchange pleasantries with the other diners. If there had been babies to kiss, he would have damn well kissed them.

Inside the kitchen, he shook hands with the chef and line cooks.

The owner, with his thin lips and bug eyes, was instantly at his side.

"Mr. Orozco, it is always a great night when you visit my restaurant."

Orozco ignored him and plucked a French fry off a plate held by a passing server.

"Aw, yes, the parmesan truffle fries are my favorite. Please include those in my meal tonight."

"Yes, of course," the owner said, glancing at a busboy who scrambled to get a plate of the fries. "We will send them to your table immediately."

The head chef pointed to a thick slab of steak sitting on a cutting board. "This is the Wagyu beef I was telling you about. The order of Miyazakigyu arrived this afternoon. The cow was killed this morning in Miyazaki Prefecture in Japan."

"Excellent," Orozco said.

"Please sample the turtle soup that will start the meal. It is my favorite."

Another cook ladled a soup spoon out of a crock.

Orozco blew gently on the soup and then tasted it.

"You have outdone yourself again," he said to the head chef.

"We will serve the first starter at your command," the chef said. "Will the younger lady be joining you and Mrs. Orozco?"

Orozco shook his head. "No. She is gone. And I'm sure she would not appreciate the subtle flavors of your genius."

The chef accepted the compliment with a slight bow.

"Besides," Orozco said as he headed for the door leading back to the dining room, "she is the main reason your freezer is fully stocked tonight."

The chef's face turned beet red.

As Orozco passed the freezer, he paused. The restaurant owner, who had been nervously hovering behind Orozco the entire time, made a small sound.

"Open it," Orozco said, and looked at the freezer door.

When the owner hesitated, Orozco laughed. "Don't worry." He patted his stomach. "I have a stomach of steel. Nothing can ruin my appetite."

The owner's face drained of color as he swung the door open.

Orozco stood for a minute and took in the view.

Right below a shelf full of canned tomatoes, beans, and broth was a tall stack of bodies. The bank manager's headless body was balanced on the top.

Orozco nodded at the sight, his face expressionless. "Didn't I say nothing could ruin my appetite? That's not entirely true. When people betray me, I do lose the desire to eat until wrongs are righted. But once they pay for it, like these men have, my appetite returns in full."

The owner swallowed hard as he closed the freezer door.

As Orozco walked out the swinging kitchen doors, the owner leaned over and retched into a large trash can.

16

Sweat poured down the sergeant's face.

"Yes. Yes. I understand."

He hung up and mopped at his face with one sleeve. An officer hunched over papers at a desk looked up.

"You okay?" the officer asked.

The sergeant ran over to get a large set of keys from a hook.

"I'm taking the big prisoner to the north wing." His voice was frantic and he was shaking.

The officer stood from behind his desk. He frowned.

"Was that the chief?"

The sergeant shook his head.

"Orozco?" the officer said in a loud whisper, and looked around quickly.

The sergeant shook his head again and made for the door.

"Someone higher? The president?"

"I have to go!" He walked out, leaving the officer standing there with his mouth open.

The sergeant nervously twisted his long mustache with one hand as he walked toward the holding cell where Shepherd had been deposited.

The cell block was eerily quiet. None of the inmates were yelling or mocking him. If Shepherd was dead, that meant he was dead, too. He began to run.

One inmate broke the silence with an odd comment as he passed. "Careful or you'll be next, *pendejo*."

He wasn't sure what the man meant until he stopped in front of Shepherd's cell.

It took him a few blinking seconds to figure out what he was looking at, and when he did, his hand holding the cell key started to shake wildly.

Shepherd sat alone on the bench at the rear of the cell. His bald head was bowed and his huge hands, still cuffed, hung between his spread knees. He didn't look up. Scattered on the concrete floor around him were the sprawled bodies of ten men. At first, the guard thought they were dead, but then he saw one man's leg twitch and heard another moan. Chavez was slumped against one wall, head lolled back, chest moving up and down.

The guard quickly muttered, "*Dios mio!*" and made the sign of the cross.

It took all his willpower to unlock the cell door, but he knew if he didn't follow Dominguez's orders, his fate would be much worse than that of the unconscious men on the floor.

As the door slid open, Shepherd stood and, without a word, walked right by the guard. He stopped in the hall, waiting silently, towering over the sergeant.

"This way," the sergeant said, trying to regain control despite his shaking voice.

Another inmate across the way muttered in a stage whisper, "Dude's going to the north wing. Adios, man. Nobody ever comes back from there."

Shepherd didn't respond. He continued walking with the sergeant behind him through a series of dank hallways and doorways. The last hallway they entered was devoid of inmates—a line of empty cells.

When the heavy door was opened, rats scurried away from the light pouring in from the hallway.

A strange smell filled the empty cell block. Not feces, piss, and sweat, like the other cells. This stench was something much worse.

Death.

The sergeant gagged slightly but tried to hide the reaction.

Shepherd paused.

"Keep going. Last cell," the sergeant said, keeping one hand on his pistol.

The cell door creaked open and Shepherd stepped inside.

The sergeant's shoulders relaxed when the bars slid shut between him and the mammoth prisoner.

Shepherd held his handcuffed wrists up to the bars, making eye contact with the sergeant for the first time. This time, a key was slid through the bars, and the handcuffs were released and dropped to the ground. Shepherd gave them a slight nudge with his foot, sliding them out the bottom of the bars. The sergeant started to pick them up but stopped, instead using his boot to scoot them further away from Shepherd's cell before he scooped them up, turned, and left.

The steel door closed behind him with a finality that echoed throughout the empty block.

Shepherd turned to examine his new home. No bench. No bed. No toilet. Nothing except four walls covered in dried blood and feces. He looked up at the ceiling. No light bulb. He looked down. His forehead scrunched in confusion. Something was written smack dab in the middle of the cracked concrete floor. The ink looked fresh. Shepherd moved closer to read the words.

Danger! Stand back by the bars.

Immediately, Shepherd threw himself backward as he heard a metallic clang on the ground near the writing.

Shepherd braced himself, throwing one meaty forearm in front of his face right before a terrific explosion ripped through the floor, showering the cell with chunks of concrete, dirt, and debris. When the dust settled, Shepherd brushed debris off his head and looked at the hole in the floor where the writing used to be.

He stepped forward and peered down into the hole warily.

A man with a dirt-streaked face looked back at him. A light on his miner's helmet shone right in Shepherd's face. After the man had turned his head so the light wasn't in his eyes, Shepherd saw that the man was standing on a pump-held railroad cart. A trail of tracks led away behind him.

"Hurry," the man said with a thick Spanish accent.

Shepherd eyed the man on the cart, sizing up the situation.

In the background, a series of sirens erupted and Shepherd heard men shouting.

Casting a last glance behind him, Shepherd dove into the hole and landed on top of the cart as the man pumped the handle furiously, his eyes now wild with fear. The cart plowed into the darkness with only the lamp from the man's hat faintly illuminating the way.

Behind them, from the cell, Shepherd heard men shouting.

Right before they rounded a corner, there was a kamikaze-like yell. Shepherd turned and saw one of the prison guards drop through the hole, his automatic rifle already firing. The rounds struck the soft dirt of the tunnel wall a few feet from them just as the handcart disappeared around a bend and plunged into fresh darkness.

17

The stark desert sunlight momentarily blinded Shepherd as the handcart rocketed out of the dark tunnel. Shepherd, who had taken over operating it, blinked as his eyes adjusted to the brightness of the surrounding Juarez Valley desert, known to locals as Murder Valley.

Even though the sun was low on the horizon, the desert was ablaze with light and heat. Sun baked the sand, sending rippled translucent waves up from the ground and blurring the surrounding landscape. Shepherd realized they had emerged into the middle of a shrub-flocked wasteland with nothing else around for miles.

Sweat poured off Shepherd as he continued to furiously pump the handle of the handcart. The miner, who had temporarily dozed off, stood up in alarm and began to speak and gesture wildly. Too late, Shepherd saw what the other man was warning him about—the tracks came to an abrupt halt, disappearing into the sand. At the last second, both men tried to brace themselves as the handcart slammed to a bone-shuddering stop. After they regained their footing, the man smiled at Shepherd and gave a small bow. Shepherd nodded grimly. "Looks like this is my stop," he said.

He climbed down from the cart. The miner turned a lever and pumped the handle of the handcart, heading back toward the tunnel, which was a looming dark spot on the horizon behind them.

Within a few moments, the cart disappeared underground, leaving Shepherd alone in the desert. He surveyed the landscape around him, shading his eyes to determine which way he should head. If the tunnel dumped him north of the jail, as he suspected, if he continued heading north he would eventually hit the border of the United States, where El Paso awaited.

Once he got there, he'd have a whole new set of problems, but crossing the border was his only option. He wasn't keen to be caught in the wilderness by narcos or federales on patrol.

Eyeing the sun, he realized he had to hustle to avoid trudging through the sand during the cold desert night. He'd done it before, in even less hospitable environments, but that didn't mean he wanted to do it again if he had a choice.

As he walked, the sun dipped lower on the horizon and Shepherd grew weary. His body was still stinging from the blows he absorbed during his arrest and later, in the jail. The sweat dripping down his temple sent a chill down his back as the desert heat began to dissipate. His pace had slowed as he headed toward a cluster of cackling vultures swarming a dead creature several feet in front of him.

At the same time the vultures cawed and scattered nervously, Shepherd heard the rumble of an engine. He paused. The sound grew louder. The vultures took flight. Shepherd was now upon the dead animal. It looked like it might have been a coyote, and the vultures had done a good job stripping the carcass of its flesh. Keeping his eyes on the slight hill in front of him, Shepherd kneeled and reached for a jagged shard of leg bone.

Legs spread, sharp bone held to his side, Shepherd planted his feet in the ground and faced the hill as the sound grew louder. A black SUV popped over the top of the hill and headed straight toward him.

He watched it grow closer with steely-eyed intensity, all feelings of fatigue instantly evaporated as he braced for another battle. His eyes narrowed as the vehicle grew closer. All the windows were darkly tinted so he couldn't see inside. But he imagined a slew of cartel hitmen loading their rifles, getting ready to throw open the doors, and either assassinate him right there or take him somewhere to torture him with a fate worse than death.

He vowed to make sure the battle ended right then and there, even if it meant the vultures returned that very night to feast on his own flesh and blood.

Resolved to fight to the death, Shepherd gave a slight nod and drew back his shoulders as the SUV skidded to a stop in front of him, sending sand scattering in a small wave.

The dark window squeakily slid down in what felt like slow motion to Shepherd.

He held his breath.

Then he saw long dark hair, huge black sunglasses, and red-painted lips.

Lucky.

Shepherd dropped the bone and asked, "Why are you here?"

"He sent me," she said.

"He?"

"Max," she said.

She threw open the driver's side door and marched across the sand toward him. She stood before him with her hands on her hips, looking up at him.

"Do you know how long I prepped for that job? A month. And you almost blew it."

"I've been prepping for two months. I've been lying low waiting for the call. I was told it was a bank job and I'd be providing additional security for a hit team." He shook his head. "And then I saw you. They knew better than to tell me *you* were the hit team."

"I don't believe you," Lucky said, and narrowed her eyes. "Max never mentioned you were going to be there."

"You actually spoke to Max?"

"I always speak to Max," she said. "Don't you?"

He shook his head. "I always speak through Red. He's my contact at The Foundation."

"Who in the hell is Red?" she said. "Your handler?"

"Very funny."

"The only thing funny is you having a babysitter."

"Listen, I'm not the one who needed backup," he said, his face growing red.

"Screw you," she said.

"Screw you."

"Don't you dare talk to me like that!" she shouted.

"You said it first," he protested.

But it was too late.

She was upon Shepherd in a second. Before he knew what hit him, a firm left uppercut struck his jaw, jerking his head back slightly.

It had been a long time since a punch had taken him that much by surprise, which was the only reason he even reeled back at all, he told himself.

But the attack didn't end there.

Lucky whipped off a silky scarf from her neck and looped it over his head. Before he could react, she'd used the material to yank his head down closer to her level and head-butted him. While he was reeling and off balance, she kicked him in the solar plexus, which sent him stumbling back before he could regain his footing. While he was off balance, Lucky launched herself onto him and held, sending him falling onto his back.

Lucky straddled him and began raining blows on his face and head, which he deflected with his beefy forearms. Then, in one smooth move, he flipped them both so that Lucky was on her back. She attempted to hit him with the blade of her palm, but he warded off the blows with his arms. Then her legs came up on the sides and she wrapped them around his lower back while hooking her elbows around his head.

Shepherd scrambled to his feet with Lucky clinging to him and tried to pry her off as she dug her elbows into his shoulder blades. He tucked his arms up through hers and flung her off. She went flying and landed with a thud on the sand a few feet away.

Gasping, she leaped up and charged him. She straddled him and looped her arm around his neck in a triangle chokehold.

Shepherd's eyes bulged but he managed to croak out some words even as he lost oxygen. "I remember this position being a lot more pleasurable the last time I saw you."

"That was then. This is now. Things change," she said, panting heavily.

Then she released her grip, rolling off of him. They lay side by side in the sand, looking up as the orange sky faded into a velvety deep blue pricked with silver stars.

They both were quiet for a few seconds as they caught their breath.

"What are you so pissed off about, anyway?" Shepherd finally asked.

"You know why!" Lucky said. "You act like I need rescuing. I don't. I don't need backup. And I don't need you. You almost blew my job. It was my job. My crew."

"Come on, Lucky," Shepherd said, sitting up and reaching for her hand to pull her to a sitting position beside him. "You know if I hadn't been at the bank, you'd be dead. Your body would be stacked at some morgue along with the rest of your crew."

Lucky winced at the mention of her crew. As they both stood and brushed themselves off, Lucky said, "The mission isn't over yet. Orozco's still out there."

Shepherd wiped the sweat and blood from his face. He leaned over and tried to wipe a smear of blood off Lucky's cheek but she swatted his hand away.

"I heard you were sitting at a restaurant with him. Why didn't you take your shot then?" he asked.

Lucky frowned. "I'm following orders. You should try it sometime."

He shrugged.

"Besides, we all know that killing him isn't enough," she said. "He's like a planarian."

"A plan what?"

"A planarian is a little, dark-loving flatworm that lives in the bowels of the earth," she said. "If you cut off its head, the head grows back. If you cut off its tail, the tail grows back. Orozco Jr. is like the head of his cartel; cut his head off and someone will replace him and other families will suffer just like mine."

"If that's the case, then what's the move, Lucky?"

She pressed her lips together tightly for a second. "I think Max wants us to take down the entire goddamn cartel."

She turned without a word and headed back toward the idling SUV.

Shepherd stood stock still.

At the vehicle, she opened the driver's side door. Before she climbed inside, she paused and turned toward him. "You coming?"

He looked back at the unforgiving desert he had just traversed, then shrugged and gave a wry smile. "Guess it beats walking."

After he climbed into the SUV, Lucky pulled on her sunglasses. They were broken in the fight so they sat crookedly on her face. She glanced over at Shepherd, who winced as he tugged on his seat belt.

She eyed him more carefully.

"Looks like you made some new friends during your short stay in Casa de Juarez Jail."

"Seems to happen everywhere I go," he said.

Lucky nodded and gunned the engine, sending the SUV barreling across the desert as the sun dipped below the horizon in the rearview mirror.

18

"Nice place you got here," Shepherd said, eyeing the hovel of a motel room. "I thought they said you were staying in a place with gold doors in Campestre."

"That place got burned when the bank job went bad."

"It went bad?"

"Thanks to you," she said, removing a hot pink sequined dress from a shopping bag.

Shepherd put up his hands, palms facing her. "Whoa. It was going bad before I even popped my head up on the scene. I saved your ass. Just like I was supposed to."

Lucky didn't argue, but made a face as she examined the dress.

"Playing dress-up?"

"So are you." She tossed him a black T-shirt and pants. "You're my security tonight. I wasn't sure what size to get so I told them something that would fit Mr. Universe."

"That's more like it," he said, and flexed his biceps.

She laughed, then looked at him. "Why don't you shower first. I think you need one more than me."

He sniffed under his arms. "Yeah. I do."

After walking over to the bathroom door, he paused and turned toward her.

"Don't suppose I get a thank you for saving you today?"

She made a face and he laughed.

Entering the bathroom, Shepherd stripped off his bloody, dirty T-shirt and stuffed it in the trash can.

His back was to her as he leaned over to turn on the shower, displaying the scars running the length of his otherwise smooth skin. Her breath caught in her throat a little. She knew all of those scars intimately. She'd patched up a few of them herself.

When they'd first met, he'd only had one scar on his back.

An unbidden memory flashed before her.

Shepherd closed the bathroom door and Lucky was thrust back in time to when she'd first met him in Kabul.

A military helicopter had whisked the two of them away from the rubble of the bombing. As they rose high above the scene, all Lucky could think about were the children who had been murdered by the US government.

As if reading her thoughts, the soldier beside her leaned over and said, "I swear to God I had no idea."

She glared at him.

"Your government kills children."

His eyes narrowed. "I know it's hard to believe, but I'm even more upset than you."

He bit out the words. She could see from his face he was telling the truth.

"Where are they taking us?" she asked. "Why did they insist on bringing me? I'm a volunteer."

He frowned. "They're going to whitewash this whole thing."

"What?" she shrieked.

"They screwed up and they are going to ask us to keep it under wraps. Otherwise, it's an international incident."

Lucky crossed her arms. "I will not be bullied by the US government."

An armed soldier across the helicopter was watching them.

Shepherd moved his body between the soldier and Lucky and leaned down.

"I'm not going to tell you what to do," he said in her ear. "But I have a plan."

"What's that?" she asked.

"We agree to whatever they ask. And then we blow the lid off this shit."

Her eyebrow rose. "How are we going to do that?"

"I got a friend. She works for Al Jazeera. She'll get the word out. I already sent her pictures from my phone and told her to sit tight. But you have to agree to everything they say and act like the bombing was good. Justified. Even throw in something about one of the kids you were helping trying to kill you. Maybe something about the whole family being dangerous terrorists."

"You're kidding me?"

"Listen, if you don't," he said, "they're going to come looking for you when these photos leak. You gotta do this to save your ass. I promise you, they will pay for this, but you've got to do what I say."

"I don't know. I don't care if they come after me," she said. "Why should I trust you anyway?"

He stared at her for so long she had to look away.

Finally, he sighed.

"If you give the slightest indication that you know it was a bad drone strike, then they are going to start covering their ass right now," he said. "We have to play along so they relax and think they are the only ones who know about this. You're going to have to act your ass off. Like Academy Award-winning shit, okay?"

Frowning, she pressed her lips together tightly.

An hour later, while sitting in a chair outside a closed door, she decided he was right.

When he came out of the door, he looked at her.

"Your turn," he said. "Just tell the truth."

She frowned, but then he winked.

It was hard to lie, but she knew the soldier was right. It was the only thing she could do to make sure the bastards paid for what they did. So she walked in and said what they wanted to hear, even though it made her sick: Thank God for the drone strike. Terrorists are bad. God bless America.

When she was done, they held open the door and thanked her for her service to the United States government.

She gave a tight smile as the door closed behind her.

Shepherd was slouched in the chair outside.

Without a word, they were in each other's arms.

Five minutes later, Lucky had pulled Shepherd into a store room.

It wasn't romantic. It was passionate and fierce and quick.

It was more than lust. It was a primal recognition and need for one another that cemented something between them.

A deep-seated knowing.

Before then, neither had given themselves as freely to another person.

Both had spent a lifetime determined to never do so.

But with one glance, recognition had dawned.

It had been met with ecstasy and then terror.

As quickly as they came together, they violently pushed one another away and resolved to never let it happen again.

And yet it did.

Lucky was jolted out of the memory by Shepherd's howl as he stepped under the motel shower's icy water. She reminded herself that this time would be different. She could not afford to have her attention anywhere except her all-encompassing mission.

Over the past few years, she had one quest that had kept her alive through her darkest grief. It was the one thing she lived for—and she would not rest until it was done.

19

Club Desire towered five stories above every other building on the street in downtown Nogales. Its stark, modern structure was painted bright orange, and one wall was covered with a picture of a blonde woman with cascading curls and a black feather boa draped strategically over her naked body.

A few tall palm trees sprouted up from the concrete out front. A sidewalk area was cordoned off with a black velvet rope. A thick-necked bouncer stood at the end of the rope near the door, eyeballing the men proffering fistfuls of pesos to gain entry.

Lucky pulled the low-profile sedan into an alley that ran alongside the building and gave a view of a side door.

"We're going in there." Lucky pointed at the door. A guard with an automatic rifle sat on a stool smoking a cigarette. "It's the 'party girl' entrance."

"Well, that explains the dress," Shepherd said, looking down at the tight pink sequined mini dress.

"What the hell does that mean?" Lucky punched him in the shoulder.

"Ouch." He made a face. "Nothing. Just that pink sequins aren't usually your thing."

"Just trying to make it as easy as possible for you to watch my ass this time," she responded with a smirk.

"Hey," Shepherd protested. "I've always had your back."

Rolling her eyes, Lucky glanced at her watch. "The party bus will be here any second. We go to the back of the line and say I'm late. You're my bodyguard."

"What line? They aren't going to let me in," Shepherd said, his eyes narrowing.

"We'll figure it out," Lucky responded. "Once we're in, we need to get to Guzman's penthouse on the seventh floor. That's where the safe room is. That's where the money is stashed. Once I'm in the penthouse, I'm going to need your help distracting Guzman so I have some time to break into the safe room."

"Got it," Shepherd said. "Just like that time in Angola."

"Hopefully this time goes better," Lucky said drily.

A few minutes later, a large white van with blacked-out windows pulled into the alley.

"Go time," Lucky said, and jumped out of the SUV. "Get ready to move."

Shepherd was out of the van and right behind her immediately.

They crouched as the van passed but then straightened when it stopped in front of the side door.

The door to the van slid open and a dozen young, beautiful Latina women in their late teens filed out, giggling and wearing revealing dresses. They were quickly waved into the side door flanked by two men acting as security guards.

Lucky and Shepherd ran across the street toward the door, but it was too late; the van pulled away, leaving them in the open.

At the door, the guard put up a meaty palm to stop Lucky.

Shepherd gave the guard an easy smile and said in flawless Spanish that they were late. They missed the bus because she took too long picking out her outfit. He rolled his eyes, and Lucky pouted and said, "I couldn't decide between the pink and the lavender."

The guard's face remained expressionless.

She winked at him. "Don't you think the pink dress was the way to go?"

"Give me your bag," he said.

Lucky opened the zipper on the small bag that hung across her body on a thin strap.

He poked around inside, took out a lipstick, and opened it, then put it back and rummaged around some more. He had a thick, round case in his hand when a woman rushed over.

She wore a white blazer over white slacks with stiletto heels and gold jewelry. Her huge black eyes took in Lucky coldly.

"They're with me," she said to the guard.

Shepherd looked up. It was the woman he helped rescue from the attacker in the alley.

The guard dropped the round compact back into Lucky's bag and undid the chain across the doorway.

Shepherd hesitated, but Lucky didn't wait for the guard to change his mind and followed the woman inside. Shepherd looked around for a second and then trailed after the two women.

Once they'd stepped inside a small alcove bordering the dance floor, Lucky stopped and turned to the woman. "Thank you."

The woman looked Lucky up and down and said, "I owe him."

Lucky raised an eyebrow, but the woman simply smiled and disappeared into the crowd.

Then Shepherd was beside her.

"That woman was stunning. She looked like a doll," Lucky said. "I take it she's a friend of yours?"

"Something like that," Shepherd said without explanation.

The girls from the bus were huddled a few feet away. Another beefy bouncer with a goatee stood with them, talking on a two-way radio.

Lucky surveyed the room. It was a dance club with disco lights, a long mirrored bar, and thumping dance music.

Only the naked or scantily dressed people crowding the bar and dance floor indicated it was a sex club.

"Looks like fun," she quipped. "Ready to mingle?"

They followed as the bouncer led the group of prostitutes and their two security guards through the crowd to the foot of a wide staircase across the dance floor.

"Let's do this," Shepherd said.

A few people stopped dancing as Lucky and Shepherd moved toward the wide staircase. A few men reached for Lucky, but Shepherd casually swatted their hands away, making Lucky snicker. One woman with bleached blonde hair and long fake eyelashes broke free of a group and planted herself in front of Shepherd, making him draw up short. She wore a thin strip of underwear, pasties over her large breasts, and nothing else. "You two are new here, no?" she said above the music. "Would you like me to show you around?"

The woman licked her lips. She swayed back and forth, unsteady on her feet. Her eyes were glazed. She'd obviously had too much to drink.

Lucky squeezed past Shepherd's shoulder and stepped between the two.

"No offense, sweetie, but you couldn't handle him," Lucky said as she grabbed Shepherd's hand and led him away from the woman. He turned and shrugged at the woman as if it wasn't his fault.

As their feet hit the stairs right behind the group of prostitutes, Shepherd leaned over and said in a low voice, "Maybe I'm mistaken, but did I just see the little green monster?"

"Hell no." Lucky made a face.

"You're jealous."

"Am not."

"Are so."

"You wish," Lucky said as they entered the second floor. "Why would I be jealous? Besides, that woman was so drunk she could barely stand. Her judgment in men might be a little off right now."

"I was talking about the woman who got us in the door."

Lucky's cheeks flared red. She didn't answer, instead taking the stairs two at a time, leaving Shepherd hurrying to catch up to her.

The stairs ended at an open space bordered by more than a dozen rooms.

In the center of the main room, half a dozen people dressed in black leather bondage gear were engaged in various dominatrix and submissive activities. A small crowd had formed around them to watch one man getting struck repeatedly with a silk whip, a woman with spiked stiletto heels stepping on a man's arms as he crawled toward her, and a woman spanking another woman who was bent over a leather bench. Beyond them were several rooms. Most contained king-size beds with people having sex on them. Each room had a mirror on the ceiling and a window where people could sit and observe from another small room.

Heads turned as the group arrived on the floor. The goateed bouncer led the young women to another staircase and Lucky and Shepherd quickly followed.

The third floor was lined with playrooms—red velvet curtains parted to reveal an alcove padded in red leather; a large room with a massive leather swing as its focal point being enjoyed by a threesome; and a dungeon room with several human-sized cages and a wall of torture accoutrements, such as handcuffs, whips, and balls on leather straps.

Every room was occupied.

This time there was no staircase, just an elevator guarded by two men with automatic rifles. Lucky jutted her chin in that direction, and Shepherd reached behind him for her hand. She ignored it and walked in front of him, joining the group just as the huge elevator slid open.

The group filed in and the door closed.

The elevator opened up to a smaller area vibrating with thumping techno music. No talking was possible, and the bouncer looked at the group and pointed to a door across the space.

This area was mostly filled with well-dressed men with obnoxious gold jewelry and naked women servicing them.

Spreading his arms wide, the bouncer stood back and motioned for the group to walk over to the door. Lucky was caught up with the women while Shepherd and the other security guards were stopped by the bouncer.

The door to the VIP penthouse opened and the young women filed in. Lucky hesitated briefly, glancing back to where the bouncer had stopped Shepherd. He gave her a look above the crowd right before she disappeared inside and the door closed.

"I'm security. I need to go in with them to protect them," he told the bouncer.

The goateed man scoffed. "We are inside Alejandro Guzman's penthouse," he said. "They are the most protected they have been in their miserable little lives."

Shepherd's eyes narrowed and his jaw tightened, but he didn't respond.

"Go wait with the other guards." The bouncer pointed to a spot at the bar where the guards had taken seats and started drinking.

Just then the bouncer's radio crackled and he looked at a camera above them. Instinctively, Shepherd bowed his head to keep his face off camera. At the same time, another bouncer shoved him in the back. "Go on."

His hands clenched into fists, Shepherd refrained from turning and taking the man out. Instead, he walked toward the bar to join the other guards.

He was almost there when he felt a hand cup his shoulder and instantly tensed.

His cover was blown. He steeled himself for a fight.

But when he turned, the bouncer was smiling at him.

"Plans have changed," the man said. "You can go inside."

Shepherd was wary but didn't hesitate. At the door, the guards parted and let him inside Guzman's lair.

As soon as he entered, he clocked all the security cameras, keeping his head bowed as he moved to catch up to the group of young women. As he walked, he pulled a pair of dark sunglasses out of his pocket and donned them, doing a quick tactical survey of the penthouse, counting the number and location of the security team, the weapons they possessed, and all possible exit points.

He followed as the group was led inside yet another room. He saw the top of Lucky's dark head toward the front. This time as the women entered, loud cheers erupted. This room was smaller, more intimate. Cartel men in cowboy-cut silk shirts and gold chains were drinking and singing along loudly to a narcocorrido song about El Chapo's exploits. Several grapefruit-sized piles of cocaine were scattered on a mirrored coffee table. Shepherd moved to an empty wall and stood with his back to it, assuming a guardlike position.

The young women were immediately surrounded by cartel men commenting on their bodies and offering them drinks.

Lucky briefly met Shepherd's eyes above the crowd, turning her head to look both directions and then back at him, raising one eyebrow.

He knew immediately what she was signaling.

Where was Guzman? He gave the slightest shrug before she turned and plastered a smile on her face as one man touched her arm. Shepherd tensed, cracking his knuckles and practicing some deep breathing.

This time when she looked over at him, he gave the faintest nod behind her. She turned her head slightly and saw a door. As they looked, the door opened and a slender man with short gray hair, a neatly trimmed goatee, and a dark blue suit emerged. The door closed before Shepherd could glimpse anything inside the room.

The man in the suit headed straight toward Shepherd, the crowd parting seamlessly as he walked. He stopped before Shepherd, looking him over from head to toe before smiling at him like the bouncer had.

"This way, please," he said.

Shepherd walked after him.

As they passed Lucky, she gave him an alarmed look.

"I'm supposed to watch the girls," Shepherd told the man when they stopped in front of the door across the room.

The door opened automatically and the goateed man held out his arm, indicating that Shepherd should enter first.

Shepherd entered, and right before the door closed, the man in the suit said, "Mr. Guzman has taken a liking to you."

"A liking?"

That same smile. "Yes. He has a very particular appetite when it comes to his pleasures, and he thinks you will do just fine."

20

Guzman's inner sanctum was lined with black and gold wallpaper. An ornate chandelier hung in the center of the room. On a wall near the door, a big-screen TV was airing the Mexican National Football team's game. A guard stood in each of the room's back corners. On the far wall was a steel-reinforced door with a security panel where a third guard stood, his automatic rifle hanging on a strap across his chest.

A massive jacuzzi on a raised platform sat on one side of the room and a fully stocked bar flanked the opposite wall.

All told, there were four other people in the room —the three guards and Guzman himself.

The drug lord sat with his arms and hairy, tree-trunk legs spread on a massive gold velvet couch.

At first glance, he appeared naked because his ample stomach hung over his navy silk boxer shorts. He had a small, wiry mustache, and his thinning black hair showed pinkish scalp despite an attempt at a combover. His thick tongue rolled across his teeth and his deep-set black eyes gleamed as he appraised Shepherd, who stood just inside the doorway.

He lifted two sausage-like fingers and gestured for Shepherd to come closer.

Shepherd complied, stopping about ten feet before the drug lord.

"Dance for me," Guzman said in Spanish.

Shepherd cocked his head, unsure that he'd heard correctly.

"And take off your shirt," Guzman added.

Shepherd's eyes flickered to the guards, who remained expressionless, their gazes straight ahead.

"What are you waiting for?" Guzman said. "Do you know who I am?"

When he didn't move or respond, one of the guards fixed his steely gaze on Shepherd and jiggled his automatic rifle.

"I know who you are," Shepherd said in a neutral voice.

The man smiled. "Then you also know that I never ask twice."

Giving a slight nod, Shepherd tugged at the hem of his form-fitting black shirt and lifted it over his head. Guzman's beady eyes tracked the movement as tanned muscles were slowly exposed. As he watched Shepherd remove his shirt, Guzman's mouth opened slightly and he inhaled sharply, making a soft sound.

After a few seconds in which Guzman lasciviously eyed Shepherd, he turned to one of his guards, who leaned over and turned a dial on a sound system.

The pulsing, sensual beat of Nine Inch Nails' "Closer" filled the small space with Trent Reznor's voice chanting about letting him violate and desecrate someone.

Without hesitation, Shepherd began to undulate his body.

For such a large man, he was surprisingly agile, and gyrated his hips and rolled his shoulders. When the song ended, Shepherd turned to the guard. "What else you got?"

Guzman guffawed and clapped his hands. The guard snickered and put on Right Said Fred's "I'm too sexy."

Now, Shepherd was arching his muscled biceps and clasping his hands behind his head as he dipped to the ground and back up, going full Magic Mike.

As he danced, he moved closer and closer, inching within striking range of Guzman.

The obese cartel man shifted on the couch and was now leaning forward, elbows on his knees, eyes glued on Shepherd. When Shepherd stopped a few feet away, Guzman crooked a finger at him to come closer.

At first, one of the security guards stepped away from the wall, but Guzman held up a palm and the man retreated. When Shepherd leaned over and playfully pushed Guzman back against the cushions, the security guards relaxed and leaned into their posts at the same time they shot each other looks of annoyance. They clearly had seen this show before.

Shepherd noticed the guards had lost interest, and so he jumped up on the couch, gyrating above Guzman's rapt gaze. Out of the corner of his eye, Shepherd saw the guards shifting from one foot to the other. Every once in a while, the room filled with cheers from the TV screen above the music.

The guards now had their eyes on the game but occasionally slanted them toward Guzman, obviously trying hard to ignore what was happening on the couch while still remaining alert.

Guzman had his hands on Shepherd's jean-clad thighs and was beginning to snake his fingers up to the jean's buttons when the television emitted raucous cheers. The guards turned their heads toward the sound.

Not squandering the split-second opportunity, Shepherd deftly spun his body and thrust his forearm around Guzman's neck in a deadly chokehold as he shouted, "Anyone moves and I'll snap his neck."

The three guards whirled, their weapons pointed at the couch. Most of Shepherd's body was shielded behind Guzman's bulk.

He leaned down slightly and whispered to Guzman, "Just how good a shot are your men? With you in front of me, they don't have much of a target when it comes to me."

Guzman instantly had sweat pouring from his temples and armpits. He rasped, "Listen to the man. Put your guns down."

The guards lowered their weapons, but Shepherd said, "Drop and kick them toward me."

Guzman nodded at his men, and they crouched to set their weapons on the floor before scooting them toward Shepherd.

"You'll never get out of here alive," Guzman said, his voice hoarse from the vise-like grip that Shepherd had on his neck.

Shepherd dragged Guzman over the back of the couch, keeping his eyes on the guards. He backed up, hauling Guzman by the neck until they were at the reinforced door to the safe room.

He swung Guzman around behind him, keeping his grip on the man's neck, and told him to open the door.

"You're dead," the drug lord managed to choke out.

Directing his attention to the guards, Shepherd lifted his chin. "You three? Out. Now."

The guards hesitated. Shepherd tightened his grip. "Tell them."

"Go," Guzman said.

One of the guards opened the door and thumping techno music filled the room. The three men filed out. Just before the door closed, a hand with red-painted fingernails grabbed it.

Lucky.

She quickly slammed the door shut behind her and jammed a wooden chair under the handle. It wouldn't hold for long. As Lucky walked over to Shepherd, she scooped up one of the guard's discarded weapons.

By the time she'd reached the opposite door, Shepherd had whipped around and was pressing Guzman's face to the retinal scanner. The drug lord struggled against it.

Maneuvering beside Guzman, Shepherd grabbed the man by the chin with one hand and used his other hand to pry open his eyelids. He then shoved Guzman's face against the retinal scanner again.

There were sounds of gunfire, loud banging, and shouting just outside the door.

Meanwhile, Lucky was attempting to grab Guzman's hand, which he kept moving out of reach. When she finally snatched his wrist, he balled his fingers in a fist to prevent Lucky from pressing his hand against the security pad. Undaunted, Lucky pried back his index finger until it snapped. He howled in pain but his hand unclenched, and Lucky slammed it against the access panel.

The door slid open. Lugging Guzman, Shepherd followed Lucky inside. They slammed the door behind them just as a small explosion blasted open the opposite door.

21

Inside the secure room lit with red emergency lights, Lucky put her hands on her hips and faced Guzman.

"Take us to the vault."

Guzman's eyes flitted to an elevator across the room.

"Yeah. Yeah. I know it's through there," she said. "We need your hand and eye to open it so get over there. I'm done playing games."

Pressing his lips together, Guzman shook his head in defiance.

In one smooth movement, Shepherd whipped out a pistol and shot Guzman in the foot.

He yelped in pain, collapsing onto the floor and grabbing at his injured foot. He'd forgotten about his broken finger until it bent awkwardly, and he screamed and held it aloft. It was now swollen and black and blue.

There were banging noises on the other side of the door as Guzman's security team tried to gain entry.

"Move it!" Shepherd shouted. "Open the elevator and take us to the vault."

"My foot hurts too much. I can't walk."

The banging grew louder.

"You're stalling!" Lucky said.

"He's slowing us down. I'll take his eye," Shepherd said. "You take his hand."

"Agreed, this guy is a waste of air." Lucky pulled a knife from a thigh holster beneath her pink sequined dress.

Guzman backed against the wall and threw up his arms as if to shield himself. Lucky took one hand and smashed his forearm against the wall. With her other hand, she pressed the knife blade against his wrist.

"Don't kill me," he cried out. "I'll open the elevator and show you a secret way out of there."

Lucky put her knife away.

Staggering slightly, Guzman walked toward the elevator, his foot leaving a trail of blood.

He activated the retinal scan and pressed his palm to the access panel. The elevator slid open. They piled inside as Guzman pushed the single button.

As the elevator dropped, Guzman cowered in the corner, fat tears running down his face and dripping onto his bare, hairy chest. When the elevator stopped, the door opened into a small room lit with blue emergency lights. A large vault sat at one end.

As soon as they walked away, the elevator door slid shut behind them. Lucky shot a worried glance behind them but hurried toward the vault.

The vault had a time lock.

Lucky turned toward Shepherd. "A small detail that Orozco failed to mention."

There was a small ding from the direction of the elevator. The display showed it had traveled back up to the fifth floor.

Guzman stood near the elevator, his arms crossed like a stubborn toddler.

"Get your ass over here and open this now," Shepherd said. "Override the time lock."

"I can't," Guzman said.

"I was afraid you were going to say that," Lucky said. From her tiny shoulder bag, she extracted the round compact the bouncer had held in his hand right before the woman in white had appeared. She flipped it open and popped out a small, round device, then stuck it to a strip of wall adjacent to the vault and twisted. It began to flash red.

"Take cover!" Lucky shouted.

Both she and Shepherd ducked into a back corner as the wall exploded, creating a large hole that revealed the inside of the vault. In the center of the room was a large wooden pallet stacked with cellophane-wrapped cash.

"How much is that?" Shepherd poked Guzman, who was covered in debris, his face white with dust.

"Two million," he said, staring straight ahead.

"That'll work," Shepherd said.

They heard a shout from the other side of the vault. Shepherd grabbed Lucky's hand and yanked her to the corner. This time Guzman fell flat to the ground and covered his head with his hands.

Seconds later, the vault's back wall and the hallway completely disintegrated in a massive, fiery explosion. While debris was still falling in chunks from the ceiling, a team of Orozco's men in helmets and heavy armored tactical gear stormed inside the vault. The entire area was now open to the back alley.

The distinct thumping of a helicopter filled the night.

The cartel men ignored everything but the pallet of cash. Working swiftly and methodically like a precision team, they secured cargo netting around the pallet. Then the helicopter was directly above, dropping a line that Orozco's men hooked to the cargo netting.

The pallet rose into the air as the men disappeared back out the hole in the wall.

Guzman's men burst out of the elevator just as Shepherd and Lucky grabbed the dangling cargo straps. They were whisked up into the air right when Guzman's men began shooting.

One of the rounds struck the strap Lucky was holding. She momentarily lost her grip and dropped, falling to the edge of the pallet, but managed to grab it instead of plunging to the ground. Acting fast, Shepherd reached down and grabbed her armpit, hoisting her up so she could get a grip on the strap again.

Then, fighting against the wash of the rotor blades, they shimmied up the cargo straps and scrambled into the helicopter, where Orozco's men awaited.

As the helicopter swooped away into the darkness, they looked down at the drug lord standing in his boxer shorts amid a massive pile of rubble. Sirens filled the air as Guzman watched his fortune disappear into the darkness.

22

Orozco's Compound

After the helicopter landed somewhere in the middle of the desert, Lucky and Shepherd were escorted into a heavily guarded walled compound.

A few men made comments about Lucky. Her mini dress was ripped on one side and covered in dust and dirt. Her feet were bare, her face was scratched, and her hair was tangled and white from dust. Shepherd didn't look much better, but at least his clothes were intact.

Inside the front door, a man in a gray hoodie took Lucky's arm and steered her toward a hallway. Another man lifted his rifle and said, "This way."

Before he headed down the other hallway, Shepherd hesitated.

Lucky stopped. "What is it?"

"Where's your necklace?" he asked.

Her face scrunched in confusion. "What?"

"Your. Necklace."

That one word said in that particular soft tone sent her hurtling back in time. A maelstrom of images flashed through her mind in a dark kaleidoscope of passion and grief:

Shepherd in the pew beside her, reaching over to adjust her necklace after it had become caught in the bodice of her lacy dress. Shepherd in a dark suit, holding one side of her father's casket as the pallbearers walked to the gravesite. Shepherd's embrace back in her childhood home when she collapsed into his arms, so overcome with grief that her legs gave out.

And then what that embrace led to ...

Shaking her head to dispel the memories, Lucky walked away from Shepherd without answering. She followed the man in the hoodie down the hall until he stopped in front of an open door. Inside was an empty barracks-type room with concrete floors, four empty bunk beds, and an attached bathroom. Bedding and clothing were stacked on one bunk.

After the door closed behind her, Lucky tried the handle. It was locked.

Eyeing the clothing, Lucky stripped out of the shredded sequined dress and headed for the shower, using a bar of soap to scrub her body raw and wash her hair. After finishing, she dried herself on the small, scratchy towel and dressed in the clothes left for her. The camouflage cargo pants were too large, but she used the canvas belt to tighten them. An oversized black T-shirt was knotted at her waist to fit better.

Then she made the bed with the fitted sheet and scratchy blanket and lay down on it to wait. Out of habit, she reached up to her collarbone to touch her necklace before she remembered it was gone.

Of course Shepherd had noticed.

After her father's funeral they had come together once again, the way they always had: in a fierce, animalistic fashion. That night it had involved broken glasses and furniture knocked over, passion bordering on violence as funeral clothes were ripped off and flung to the carpet, forging an unmistakably erotic trail to her childhood bedroom.

They never spoke about these brief, frenzied trysts.

There was nothing to say.

They didn't trust one another. Or maybe they did.

Maybe it was that they didn't trust themselves.

Lucky vowed that this time would be different. This time, they would not allow themselves to go there.

It would be better that way.

Yes, Lucky told herself as she drifted off to sleep. This time it would remain platonic.

A little later, she startled awake when the door opened and a pair of black combat boots were put inside. She sat up and tried them on. They weren't a perfect fit but they would work.

Keeping the boots on, she lay back in the bed and tried to sleep, knowing she would need to be alert for whatever would come next.

Sometime later, her door opened again. She blinked against the light streaming in from the hallway behind the silhouette of a man.

"Come," he said.

She followed him down the hall and then up a flight of stairs. When she got to the top of the stairs, she saw Shepherd waiting. He was dressed in similar clothes. She was surprised to find herself filled with relief at the sight of him.

Then she saw Dominguez with his lanky build, black sideburns, and craggy, lined face.

"This way," he said, speaking around the gold and black cigarette between his lips.

Dominguez escorted them into an office where Orozco was sitting behind a large wooden desk. Danny Chavez stood in a corner wearing a printed shirt, bootcut jeans, and scuffed cowboy boots. A revolver was tucked into a hip holster. His greasy hair was swept back from his face, making the eyeless skull tattoo between his eyebrows the only thing Lucky saw when she walked in. As soon as she saw him, she bristled.

He leered at her, revealing a mouth full of gold teeth. She met his gaze with steely-eyed indolence.

A deep-seated fury spread through Lucky's core. After years of waiting to look this man in the eyes, she was forced to restrain herself and play it cool.

His eyes then flicked to Shepherd and narrowed. Chavez raised his index finger to the bridge of his nose, where an angry line of stitches ran just below the skull tattoo. Shepherd winked at him and said, "Lookin' good."

Dominguez indicated that Shepherd and Lucky should remain standing in front of the desk. He took a post behind them near the door. On alert.

Lucky and Shepherd exchanged a look. They were not quite prisoners, but they were clearly not honored guests, either.

Lucky knew what they were to Orozco: a surprise.

She realized that Orozco had never expected to see her again.

After her eyes quickly assessed Chavez and dismissed him, Lucky took in the room.

It didn't match the rest of the compound. It was lavish, with leather and dark wood and deep carpets. With its paintings of hunting dogs and prints of ancient world maps, the office felt as if it were picked up and plucked out of an English manor. The bookshelf behind the desk contained dozens of books on leadership and war—*The Art of War*; Colin Powell's autobiography, *In My American Journey*; and *Deep Survival: Who Lives, Who Dies, and Why*.

Orozco clearly thought he was a five-star general. Or a president. Or a prime minister. Or all of the above combined.

Lucky made note of this and pulled her shoulders back.

She knew exactly what role she played: a foot soldier being sent to battle. An expendable asset. That's why he'd offered her the Guzman job. He'd never expected her to succeed. And he most certainly never expected her to walk out of there alive.

Nobody moved or spoke as they waited for Orozco to look up.

The already short Orozco seemed even smaller today as he sat in the huge leather office chair with the winged back. His full head of dark hair was bowed and his fingers riffled through a stack of papers. He scowled at the paperwork, his thick black mustache moving as he did so, but he didn't look up.

Then, after a long five minutes, Orozco sighed and lifted his eyes.

Frowning, he said, "I'm not sure how, but you have done what others in my employ have failed to do."

He paused and shot a glance at Dominguez. Lucky turned slightly and saw that Dominguez took the slight in stride, remaining stone-faced.

Orozco pushed back his chair, stood, and then paced in front of a large window overlooking a courtyard. He crooked his finger at Shepherd and Lucky. They walked over to the window and stood beside him as he faced it.

Lucky could see the top of his head. A few stray flakes of dandruff were scattered in the thick curls.

"Those are just a few of my men," he said, and pointed down at the courtyard, which was filled with about two dozen men. Despite the sweltering heat, they wore full combat gear and were marching in formation.

"Those men in the front," Orozco said, "the older men. The ones leading the rest? They were trained at your very own Ft. Bragg."

Shepherd's only reaction to this was to chew on the inside of his lip. Lucky's eyebrows drew together.

Orozco looked at her. "You don't believe me?"

Lucky shrugged.

"They were elite Mexican Airmobile Special Forces troops sent to train in the 1990s with the Snake Eaters. You probably haven't heard of them, but they are the 7th Special Forces group. The skills they learned have made them expert assassins."

Lucky gave a slight nod.

Orozco returned to his desk and sat down.

Shepherd and Lucky walked back to stand in front of his desk. Both had their hands behind their backs.

"I only share that detail to show you that I am used to having the best of the best around me. With that said, you can assume I'm not a man who is easily impressed. I don't let just anyone into my inner circle. Most people who have seen the inside of this office have never left here alive."

He paused. Lucky tensed and stopped herself from looking at Shepherd.

Then Orozco smiled. "Welcome to the family."

Lucky and Shepherd both bowed their heads slightly to acknowledge his words.

Shuffling some papers on his desk, Orozco cleared his throat and said, "I have a shipment that needs delivering. Dominguez will fill you in on the details."

When he finished speaking, he reached for a pen and bowed his head over a sheaf of papers. The conversation was over. They had clearly been dismissed.

Dominguez and Chavez made for the door.

But Lucky and Shepherd remained standing before the desk.

"Where to?" Lucky asked.

Orozco looked up and frowned as if he was surprised they were still standing there.

"Texas."

23

Border of El Paso

The eleven lanes stretched across the road heading for the US border were jam-packed with vehicles heading for the checkpoints.

Flashing LED screens directed cars and told drivers to have documents ready for inspection.

One large sign said, "Welcome to the United States."

Large skyscrapers loomed in the distance, the shiny mirrored windows reflecting the promises of America.

Lucky was looking out the passenger window at the endless stream of people walking in an area off to one side on their way to the pedestrian crossing.

"Listen, man, I'd hop on the next plane to Juarez if I were you," Shepherd said into a disposable cell phone, one arm flung casually over the truck's steering wheel. He shot Lucky an annoyed look. "It doesn't matter who I am. I just met your kid in jail. It ain't a pretty place. He's been there too long as it is."

He shook his head. "I'm sure he's a pain in your ass, but nobody deserves to be in that jail unless they are a stone-cold killer. Go get your kid while you still can."

He hung up and looked at Lucky.

"No wonder the kid is messed up. Dad is a piece of work."

"Sounds like it," Lucky said. She turned back toward the windshield, her expression unreadable behind her dark sunglasses.

Shepherd eyed the long line of cars at the border crossing. Only a few more waited in front of them. The checkpoint was inching closer. They moved into the area where the lanes were divided by yellow concrete posts.

"Almost game time," he said.

They'd been in line for forty-five minutes. The air conditioning in the ancient box truck wheezed loudly but only spat hot air into the truck's cab. Lucky had twisted her hair into a loose knot on top of her head and stuck a pencil through it to keep it intact.

The front of Shepherd's black T-shirt was soaked with sweat and his forearms glistened as he tightened his grip on the steering wheel.

His foot let up a little on the brakes as the pickup in front of him eased forward. But then the line stopped again. Five cars in front of them now.

At least one border control agent worked each of the eleven lines on foot with other agents inside the booths. Shepherd eyed the agent at the front of their line. He was tall and thin with a permanent scowl.

"I don't like this," Shepherd said.

"It's taken care of." Lucky reached for her gun. "Dominguez said the third line from the left and that's where we are. It's going to be fine."

Shepherd was about to argue when he noticed movement out of the corner of his eye. He looked over to see a woman in the passenger seat of a large RV in the next lane over. She had a short gray bob and eyeglasses. A little dog was yapping on her lap. She was looking right at Shepherd and saying something. He scrunched up his face, trying to hear, but the barking overrode anything the woman was saying. He cupped a hand to his ear and then shrugged.

She kept pointing at the side of the box truck. He frowned. He looked in his rearview mirror but couldn't see much behind him. Then he craned his neck out the window and looked at what she was pointing at. All he saw was the goofy mural painted on the box truck—a half dozen bibles with wings on them floating down from a big poofy cloud and then the words, "Heaven Sent Bibles."

When he turned back, the woman was giving him an enthusiastic thumbs up, then put her palms together as if she was praying. He smiled and then quickly turned back to the road, easing up on the brakes again as two cars quickly passed through the checkpoint. Now there was only a sedan immediately in front of them and an SUV stopped at the checkpoint. They'd be through within moments. That's when Shepherd saw that the border patrol agent was glancing back and forth from a white sheet of paper in his hands to the SUV's occupants.

He and Lucky spotted the wanted flyer at the same time. Even from two car lengths away, it wasn't hard to miss the photo of a woman with dark hair and a bald man.

"Jesus," Shepherd breathed.

"Mary and Joseph," she added, and made the sign of the cross. "Better get those bibles ready to swear on."

Reaching over, she opened a bible on the seat beside her. A Glock 42 was tucked in its hollowed-out core.

Shepherd gripped the steering wheel even tighter, the whites of his knuckles showing. Lucky was biting her lip and looking in the rearview mirror. The huge eighteen-wheeler semi-truck behind them had pulled startlingly close. There was only a foot between them and the sedan in front of them. They were boxed in.

The SUV pulled out of the checkpoint and the sedan in front of them came to a halt. The border patrol agent leaned down to speak to the occupants. Just like he had with the SUV, he glanced at the white flyer in his hand first.

Then he said something and the sedan drove forward. The guard was about to turn to face the box truck when something caught his attention from behind.

"This is bad," Shepherd said as he eased the truck forward. He nodded toward the glove box. "Do you mind?"

His gun, too large to fit in a hollowed-out bible, was tucked inside, wrapped in a towel.

"Wait." Lucky held up a palm, focused on something in front of them.

Now, they were nearly under the checkpoint roof.

The guard was still turned toward the booth. A short man loped out of the guard house and toward the tall, skinny guard. They were several feet away but Shepherd caught a snippet of the conversation, hearing the word "break." Other words were exchanged and the tall guard handed the shorter guard a white piece of paper. The shorter guard trained his gaze on the box truck and met Shepherd's eyes.

Sweat was pouring down Shepherd's temples now and his grip on the steering wheel was slippery. His gun rested in his lap where Lucky set it seconds before. She held her own gun on her lap, cocked and pointed toward the driver's side door.

The guard, who was shorter than the box truck window, looked down at the flyer and then up at Shepherd. Then he smiled, revealing a gold tooth, and stepped back to wave them through without saying a word.

24

A field outside Odessa, Texas

In the deep Texas night, the massive white tent glowed like a beacon across the vast, barren landscape.

A long, dusty dirt road led from the highway out to the revival area. Hundreds of cars were parked in the lot in front of the tent and lined both the dirt road and the highway shoulder for a good quarter mile.

A crowd numbering near a thousand filled folding chairs under the tent. Another ten rows spilled outside the tent and into the surrounding field. Large speakers were set up in the field to serve the overflow.

At the front of the tent on a small stage, Pastor Mathias Tomlinson paced, riling up the crowd, asking them if they were ready to meet the Lord on this very day.

Tomlinson wore a tight white suit with a skinny black tie that made him look like a pro wrestler playing dress-up. A black widow spider tattoo covered one side of his thick neck. The backs of both hands had tattoos of striped snakes.

His dark eyebrows stood out below his silver crew cut. His smile was wide and his face and actions animated. Now, he was speaking fast like an auctioneer, telling the crowd how the Lord Jesus was in their presence. Six women with gray hair stood in front of folding chairs behind him, singing energetic gospel music as he paced. People were standing on their chairs, waving their bibles, and shouting, "Amen!" and "Hallelujah!" and "Praise the Lord!"

Tomlinson paused suddenly and the women behind him quit singing. The crowd fell silent, waiting.

"You all can have a seat now. We're going to talk some serious stuff today," he said.

People took their seats.

"Today we're going to talk about angels."

The crowd erupted into cheering.

"I said angels, oh my Lord, I said angels, oh my God, I said angels!"

"Amens" spread through the crowd.

"Now you all know the story about how the Lord sent one of his angels to destroy the wicked? No? You don't? Well you're gonna know it now," he said. "Open up your bibles, I sure hope you brought your bibles, now open them up right now and we're gonna hear how an angel of the Lord killed 185,000 enemies of God. Yes, sirree. An angel killed those enemies of God. But don't worry, that doesn't mean you have to be afraid of angels. The Lord God I know, the alpha, the omega, the beginning and the end, he's not gonna hurt you unless, unless, you're an enemy of God."

There were boos now in the crowd.

"Are you an enemy of God?" Tomlinson raised his voice as he began pacing the stage, moving faster.

"Come on now! Come on now! You an enemy of God?"

He paused and pointed.

"Sir? You in the Rangers shirt? You saved?"

The man nodded.

Tomlinson stuck up his thumb. "Hallelujah. Glory to God. Praise God."

Now Tomlinson was in the crowd. He stopped before a beautiful woman in a floral dress and ample cleavage. She blushed as he leaned down.

"You got a sec? You saved? You wanna be? It don't hurt. I promise it won't hurt."

The women around her giggled. But she burst into tears.

"All you have to do is decide to accept the Lord Jesus right now? You ready? He'll take you out of that pig pen situation you're in and show you the light. I know. He did it for me. I'm living proof. Well you think about it and let me know after this what you think. If you're ready."

Tomlinson stalked away and took the stage again.

"All right. Now, you all aren't enemies of God or you wouldn't even be here tonight. But these folks were. So the Lord, the omniscient, omnipresent, all-knowing God, sent down his angel to show them that he meant business. That angel came down, ripped out the souls of the wicked, and flung them to the depths of hell like taking out the trash.

"Now open your bible to 2 Kings 19:35 and read along with me. It said here in the good book, 'That night the angel of the Lord went out and put to death a hundred and eighty-five thousand in the Assyrian camp. When the people got up the next morning there were all the dead bodies!' THERE WERE ALL THE DEAD BODIES," Tomlinson shouted now. "Now I don't know about you, but that's pretty dark stuff if you ask me, man. ALL THE DEAD BODIES. But that's God for you—taking out the trash!"

Amens flooded the crowd.

"Now in all seriousness, let's talk real talk here. As some of you know, I used to be one of those pieces of trash and it is only by God's grace that I stand here before you today. And now, now, I help those angels serve up a big old platter of deliverance and rip out the souls of the wicked that walk this here God's green earth.

"I personally know this as fact. We have angels walking on earth keeping us safe from the wicked. You know how I know? You want to know how I know that this is fact? I'll tell you. I personally know one of these warriors out there fighting the good fight. I know a warrior who is out there eradicating the wicked. You all know what eradication is, right? According to the dictionary, it means to permanently remove something, to pull it up by the roots, to do away with completely. And the example they give is, 'The disease has been completely eradicated.'"

The crowd clapped and cheered.

Tomlinson paused and smiled.

"Now you all know I preach about the disease that is taking over our country. Men who are in league with the devil."

"Amens" erupted again.

"Oh yeah, I went there all right. I said it. I own it. Other preachers won't tell you, but I'm gonna tell you: the men running this country are in league with the devil. They can't even prove they're Americans. They can't even prove they were born in this country. Our very own president looks like he came over here in a boat last week."

People in the audience burst into clapping and cheers.

"They don't want to support the good, hardworking people who founded this country. The hardworking Americans whose ancestors have been here for centuries. They just come over here to our country and take what we've worked hard to establish and govern it all willy-nilly. And in the process? They want to stomp you down. They want to destroy our country. Man, they even want to eradicate people like me who are out here telling the truth."

More boos spread through the crowd. Now, Tomlinson was bent over, running up and down the aisles, pointing his finger and gesticulating.

"I'm going to tell you a story. I'm gonna tell you about what one man did for me. I wasn't always this holy, oh Lord, let me tell you."

The crowd laughed.

"I was a hoodlum. A drugged-out piece of trash. And one night I was desperate for drugs. But I had no money. But I was a slave to those drugs. So I did what I did in those days and I waited outside a fancy restaurant and saw a man walking over to his fancy old car. And I walked up and I said, 'Give me your money.'

"And this man, he just looked at me and said, 'Son, you've had a rough life, haven't you?' And you know what I said? You know what I said?"

The crowd screamed, "What?"

Tomlinson paused dramatically and leaned down to one woman in an aisle seat. "Do you know what I said?"

"No, Pastor Tomlinson," she said.

"I'll tell you what I said. I said, 'Shut up.'"

The crowd laughed.

"Then that man said, 'You know, I don't think you want to be out here in the cold waiting to rob someone of their money.'

"'The hell I don't,' I told him. He shook his head and said, 'No. You don't. It's just that you've tried everything else in life and nothing's worked, has it?' I was pissed right then because that man didn't know me but he knew me. He said those words and they spoke straight to my soul. But I still hated him right then. Then he said, 'You tried everything and nothing worked, why don't you try the Lord.'

"I said, 'How about I try whooping your butt if you don't give me money right now'—except you all know I didn't say whooping and I didn't say butt."

The crowd, leaning forward now, hanging on his words, laughed.

"This man said, 'Go ahead and try to whoop my butt. See if the Lord will let you.'"

Tomlinson walked back to the stage.

"I spit on the ground and I reared back and got ready to punch his lights out. You know what?"

"What?" the crowd shouted.

"I couldn't do it. I could not raise my fist against that man. I wanted to. Oh, Lord knows I wanted to. Instead, I got down on my knees and I cried. And he said, 'Get up, son! I ain't the Lord. Don't pray to me. I'm just the messenger.'"

More laughter.

"Then this man invited me to his church that night. And I went. I actually went. And I ain't never been the same. Two days after that, my buddy used the heroin I was going to buy and he died from it. It was a bad batch. And I would've been the one to die. But this man saved me that night. I was called!" Tomlinson was yelling now, pacing the stage at a frenetic rate and speaking faster and faster. "And I found God—and myself—thanks to this man. He set me free."

The crowd was in a fervor, shouting, "Amen!" and waving their bibles in the air.

Tomlinson suddenly stopped in the middle of the stage and was silent.

The crowd grew quiet.

"Now I bet you're all wondering who this man is? Right? I know you are. Well just so happens this is a very special day today. That man, that man who took me to his church, he's right here. And he's gonna change the world. He's the one who's going to eradicate the wicked just like that angel of the Lord did so long ago. Now this man is like that angel. Would you like to meet him? I'd like to introduce him to you. Come on out now."

A thin man with a thick head of wavy blond hair wearing a light blue suit and red tie walked onto the stage. He had a ruddy but handsome face and a gleaming white grin like a young Robert Redford. He shook Tomlinson's hand heartily and then waved and smiled at the crowd.

"Folks, it is my pleasure to introduce you to Bill Crenshaw," Tomlinson said. "You might have seen his pictures on posters in town. He's our gubernatorial candidate. He's going to bring Texas to the attention of the nation, and then he's gonna take us to the promised land—the White House! You don't want to miss his speech tomorrow at the convention center. But I wanted to personally introduce him to you and to tell you that this man is gonna need your help if he's gonna save this country single-handedly. He needs you."

Crenshaw briefly took the microphone. "Now Pastor Tomlinson is a tough act to follow so I'm not going to take up any time tonight except to say hello and I hope to get to see you and talk to you tomorrow at the convention center. I've got a lot of concerns I want to share with you and tell you my plans to fix what's wrong with this country. Thank you and God bless you!"

People in the crowd cheered, whistled, and screamed.

Tomlinson waited for them to quiet down, then took the microphone again.

"Now, you can see my friends out there in the white shirts passing around the collection basket? Well, I'm asking you to search your hearts when you open your wallet or your pocketbook and remember that this man is gonna need your help to make sure that God's Hand can once again sit up on the throne and cast out the wicked."

Headlights flashed in the distance. Tomlinson looked out over the crowd and saw the Heaven Sent Bible truck turn onto the dirt road leading to the tent.

Crenshaw saw it too.

"Goodnight, folks," Tomlinson said into his mic. "Don't forget to dig deep. We need to eradicate the wicked. This is a holy calling right here. God bless you all. Amen."

The two men walked to the back of the tent escorted by Tomlinson's bodyguard, Kong.

Kong was bald with a thick brown goatee that was about six inches long. He wore a sleeveless muscle tee and his body was dark with tattoos from the sides of his head to his fingernails. A large swastika with the words "Aryan Brotherhood" written in a semi-circle underneath took up most of his neck on the right side.

A crowd tried to follow them as they headed to the back of the tent. People screamed and shouted and asked for Tomlinson to place his hands on them and heal them. The two men ignored them and entered a narrow walkway leading to a gate and, beyond that, a small trailer. Kong stood in front of the waist-high gate, deterring anyone who might want to crawl over it.

Tomlinson looked back briefly and saw the young woman who had been wearing the flowered dress. She was leaning toward him, reaching out her hands and smiling now. Tomlinson eyed her ample cleavage and leaned over to whisper to Kong, "Send her back when we're done with our business."

Then he winked at the woman and walked away.

25

After poking his head out the back of the tent door and looking around, Kong motioned for the two men to follow him. He then led Tomlinson and Crenshaw outside and then around a large eighteen-wheeler parked behind the tent.

A few seconds later, the Heaven Sent box truck pulled up and parked.

Lucky hopped out first, but Shepherd was right behind her. They both eyed Kong warily.

The bodyguard motioned Tomlinson forward out of the shadows. About six men filed out of the tent and stood near Kong. The huge bodyguard's mouth twitched under his brown goatee. He flexed his muscles, rotated his neck, and cracked his knuckles as if preparing for a fistfight.

Shepherd ignored the other man completely, keeping his eyes on the preacher.

Tomlinson's steely eyes took in the other man from head to toe. Shepherd met his gaze head-on and lifted an eyebrow. The preacher ignored this and turned his attention to Lucky. This time a hungry look spread across his face and he walked in a slow circle around her. He muttered something that sounded like "wetback."

"Orozco assured me that you wouldn't have weapons," Tomlinson said, and stopped abruptly in front of Lucky, his face only inches away.

"That's right," Lucky said.

"But I don't trust Mexicans."

"She's American," Shepherd said. He started to say something else, but Lucky gave the slightest warning nod and he closed his mouth.

"So I'm gonna pat you down, okay, sugar?"

He reached for her and Lucky tensed. Her fingers twitched near her empty holster but other than that she didn't move. Kong saw the movement and gave a slow warning nod. She met his eyes but didn't respond.

Before Tomlinson touched her, he turned to Crenshaw. "You want in on some of this action?"

The other man gave a nervous laugh. "Maybe next time," he said.

Then Tomlinson grazed his fingers along her jawbone. Lucky turned her head slightly toward Shepherd. The vein on the side of Shepherd's neck was throbbing and the muscle in his jaw twitching. Quickly, she snapped her teeth together and Tomlinson jerked back his hand.

"Fiery one, aren't you?"

"You have no idea," Lucky said, and cocked one eyebrow.

Stepping back, Tomlinson stood in front of the pair, rubbing his palms together and smiling. He shed his sport coat and handed it to one of the men behind him without turning around. Then he loosened his tie and unbuttoned his shirt.

His defined chest was hairless and sported white supremacist tattoos, including a large one across his chest that read, "I kill Mexicans."

Lucky's face remained expressionless.

"Orozco said he was sending someone new," Tomlinson said. "Why you two?"

"You're an important man," Lucky said. "That's why."

Tomlinson's eyes narrowed as he tried to figure out if she was being disrespectful. Then he gave a broad smile and wiped the sweat off his brow with a thick forearm.

"It's hotter than a whore in church out here." He licked his lips suggestively, leaning in toward Lucky's face. "Let's quit piddlin' around and get this over with."

Shepherd went to the truck and threw up the rolling door. Neat stacks of bibles filled the truck bed.

Kong nodded, and the six men walked over to the truck and began carrying stacks of bibles to the open trunk of a limo parked nearby. Crenshaw paced near his limo, biting at his inner lip.

While the transfer occurred, Tomlinson came over and stood next to Lucky, so close his thigh touched hers. She didn't shrink away but also didn't look at him, keeping her eyes on the transfer operation.

Tomlinson watched her, his face only inches away. He reached out and snatched a bible from a stack as one of the men passed by.

He opened it to reveal a neat brick of cocaine nestled inside the hollowed-out interior. He looked up, and in seconds Kong was at his side with a large hunting knife. He sliced the plastic around the brick in one fluid motion. Tomlinson dipped a pinky finger with a gold ring into the cocaine, pressed it to one nostril, and sniffed. Then he shook his head and laughed, nodding at Kong.

The bodyguard walked back to the truck and clambered inside. In the back, behind the stacks of bibles, were three large duffel bags. He unzipped one and held it up toward Tomlinson. It was packed with stacks of money. He jumped out of the truck with two of the bags and headed toward the limo.

Another bodyguard was standing by the limo's back door. Kong handed him the duffel bags and the man put them in the back seat. Then Kong retrieved the third bag, this one slightly different than the other two—it was the large bag that Lucky plopped on the restaurant table for Orozco. Kong was just about to pass Lucky as he walked toward the limo when there was an unmistakable sound in the distance.

Motorcycles.

Lucky shot Shepherd a look. He gave a nearly imperceptible shrug.

As the low rumble got louder, the men transporting the bibles swore loudly and began to run, scrambling to transfer the drug-filled bibles.

Tomlinson looked around wildly. His eyes rested on Lucky and Shepherd.

Lucky raised her hands. "Not us, man."

"No shit," he said as he turned toward the limo. "It's those assholes, the 12 Locas."

Seconds later, bullets ripped into the side of the truck.

26

As people scattered and took cover, Shepherd and Lucky ducked behind the box truck with two of Tomlinson's men. Screams filled the air as churchgoers stampeded.

The bikers were now behind the tent, taking cover on the other side of the semi-truck and firing nonstop. Rounds hit the truck, the limo, and the dirt. One of Tomlinson's men near the limo dropped. Another man, near Shepherd and Lucky, poked his head out from around the side of the box truck to shoot but ended up with a round to the chest. He staggered backward before he collapsed on the ground, lifeless eyes staring up at the stars. Shepherd leaned over and grabbed the man's cowboy boot, pulling him back behind the truck so he could scoop up his semi-automatic weapon.

Now the biker gang had moved around the semi-truck and were heading right toward the limousine. Shepherd laid down suppressive fire as he and Lucky raced to take new cover.

One of the motorcyclists rounded the corner in a furious skid and let loose a full mag from a Mac 10 machine gun. Lucky was crouched behind the engine block of the truck only a few feet away. Shepherd tossed Lucky the gun, and she stood and took out the bike's front tire, sending the gunman flying into the air. It was then that she noticed something different.

The biker had on tight leggings, thigh-high boots, and a long black ponytail hung out from her helmet. Lucky looked around.

At first, because they all wore helmets and thick leather jackets, she had not noticed that all the bikers were women.

In the chaos, Kong quickly escorted Tomlinson into Crenshaw's limo. The driver peeled out, the trunk with bibles still wide open and flapping as the vehicle hit potholes and small brush in the open desert.

But the limo didn't get very far. One of the bikers raced after it, peppering its side with a flurry of bullets. One bullet struck the driver and the limo came to a stop several yards later.

Tomlinson's outraged scream could be heard over the gunfire. A biker was nearly upon the limo when Kong kicked open the door and fired one bullet, sending the woman spiraling to her death.

Another biker nearby screamed in fury and gunned her bike toward the limo in a kamikaze yell just as Kong stepped outside with a duffle bag of money. The biker fired at Kong and he dropped, clutching his side. The woman brought her bike to a sliding stop, reached down, scooped up the bag, and zoomed away.

Meanwhile, another biker had snuck up on Shepherd and was about to shoot him when Lucky noticed and pivoted, laying down a stream of bullets that sent the biker scrambling for cover.

"That's one for me," Lucky shouted at Shepherd. "We're dead even if you count the bank."

"I've got one on you," Shepherd said.

"How you figure?"

"Helicopter ride out of Guzman's club."

While her attention was turned toward Shepherd, another biker snuck around the truck and fired. Lucky dove but the bullet caught her arm. She executed a roll and was under the truck holding her shoulder when Shepherd crouched beside the truck.

Keeping his eyes on the back of the truck, he said, "You good? Lucky? Lucky?" His voice grew slightly panicked.

"Yeah," she grunted. "Sorry I didn't answer. I had my belt in my mouth. I'm making a crappy tourniquet, but I think it's just a flesh wound."

After a few seconds, Lucky shimmied out from under the truck, Army-crawl style.

A fabric belt was nodded around her bicep. Shepherd grabbed her other arm and effortlessly lifted her to a standing position. He crept to the edge of the truck and poked his head out. He fired a few times but the gun battle was slowing down amid the sounds of motorcycles rumbling away.

The last of the bikers left as sirens filled the night air.

"Let's make a break for it." Shepherd nodded at the eighteen-wheeler nearby. They raced toward the semi-truck parked behind the tent a few seconds before one of the last bikers plucked a hand grenade from her leather jacket and tossed it into the box truck as she roared past on her bike. The truck rattled with the explosion.

On the other side of the tent, Lucky and Shepherd watched as a limping Kong ushered Tomlinson and Crenshaw to a nearby dirt parking lot. Frantic parishioners were still trying to flee the chaos.

Reaching into the open window of one vehicle, Kong grabbed the elderly driver by the collar and yanked him out. He flung the man to the ground and climbed behind the wheel as the driver scrambled to his feet and ran away. Tomlinson and Crenshaw climbed into the backseat, and the car took off before Lucky and Shepherd could give chase.

They ran back around the semi-truck, looking for a way to escape.

One of the dead gang member's bikes was idling on the ground. Shepherd scooped it up and revved the engine as Lucky climbed onto the back. She gripped his waist as they headed into the dark desert.

Police squads came screaming from the nearby road to find three separate dust trails leading away from the tent.

27

The flickering light of a dying neon sign flashing "Motel" lit up the inside of the second-floor room. They'd kept the tattered curtains on the front window open so they could see if anyone had followed them. The motel building formed a U, and the second-floor rooms were accessed by an outdoor balcony overlooking the parking lot.

Lucky and Shepherd sat at a small table by the room's large window. A plastic bag on the table held the makeshift medical supplies Shepherd bought at a convenience store down the road—bandages, tweezers, a small sewing kit, and a bottle of vodka.

Lucky was leaning forward, her forearm outstretched on a stack of newspapers that lay on the table. Shepherd's head was bowed as he examined the gunshot wound, prodding at it with the tweezers.

"Ow!" Lucky said. "You digging for gold in there or what?"

Shepherd sat back with the tweezers in his hand.

"Gold? You think you need a golden bullet to be killed? Like a vampire?"

"It's a silver bullet and it kills werewolves," Lucky said.

"Right." Shepherd rolled his eyes. "Okay, I'm going to try one more time. We can't take you to the hospital so I'm the best you got. Plus, I'm really good at this sort of thing. I played Operation as a kid all the time."

"So obviously that makes you an expert?" She winced as he dug in again with the tweezers.

He plucked the bullet out and held it up for her to see. "Jackpot."

"Damn!" she said as Shepherd doused the open wound with alcohol.

"Quit being a baby," he said.

"Quit hurting me," she responded, and gave him a solid punch to his shoulder with her other hand. She winced as her knuckles hit rock-solid muscle. "Damn it. That hurt, too."

"You've gone soft, Lucky," he said.

"The hell I have," she said angrily.

Shepherd rolled his eyes. "I've seen you nearly lose your arm after a haphazard machete strike and you're telling me this hurts. A little germ killer."

"Yes!" she said, tears smarting her eyes. "By the way, I was the one who saved your ass that time even with my arm in a sling."

"Whatever." Shepherd gave a sharp tug to tighten the strip of fabric he had tied above the wound to temporarily stop the bleeding. "I saved your ass in Fallujah."

"I saved your ass in Lexington." Lucky raised her eyebrow.

"Lexington?" Shepherd said, and scrunched up his face.

"When that Delta guy was about to cave your skull in."

Shepherd scoffed. "Was not."

"Yeah, he was," Lucky said in an indignant voice. "You were hitting on his girlfriend."

Shepherd shrugged. "Yeah, but he wasn't going to do anything about it."

"The hell he wasn't!"

"He left with his tail between his legs."

"Only because I told him he wasn't going to hurt you and he believed me. I saved your ass."

"We're going to have to agree to disagree on that one."

"No way," she said, and looked down. She realized then that their lively conversation had distracted her while Shepherd had put two quick stitches into her forearm.

"Nice work," she said.

"One more to go."

Lucky closed her eyes and breathed heavily but did not protest the pain.

When Shepherd finished and she opened her eyes, he was staring at her with a strange look.

She swallowed and looked away.

Then he cleared his throat and began to clean up the medical supplies.

"You want to shower first or should I?" he said. His voice was casual, friendly, but something about it set her on edge. The one bed suddenly seemed to take up the entire room. Both had avoided it like the plague, sitting at the small table by the window since they had arrived.

"Yeah. Go for it," she said lightly.

They could sleep in the same bed and control themselves. They'd done it plenty of times on ops over the years.

Still, she watched him with slitted eyes as he walked toward the bathroom, lifting the hem of his shirt.

But then he turned back. They both heard the sound at the same time —a car pulling into the parking lot below. They walked over to the window and peered out. A woman in a mini skirt and a man in a business suit got out and stumbled toward the lobby.

They both relaxed.

Shepherd sank into the chair by the window.

Lucky took the bottle of 80 proof vodka and put it up to her mouth, taking a few long pulls before passing it to Shepherd, who did the same.

He set the bottle on the table and looked at Lucky.

"What?" She frowned.

"You're tougher than you think," he said. "I was in agony when that doctor in Kabul stitched me up without anesthesia."

"I remember," she said drily.

There were other things they both remembered about Kabul.

They stared at each other in the sudden silence.

Shepherd cleared his throat.

"I'll sleep on the floor tonight," he said.

Lucky swallowed.

The moment had passed. The shower forgotten. They were back to business.

Lucky stood and examined her arm. "Looks good, Shepherd."

Just then his phone dinged.

He held the message up to show Lucky.

It said, "12 Locas hangout" and listed an address.

"Damn, you're good," Lucky said, and then squinted as she read the phone. "Oh, never mind, it's from your babysitter, Red."

Shepherd quickly put his phone back in his pocket.

Lucky got up, stretched, and pulled on a thick black hoodie jacket. She zipped it up and reached for the door handle.

"Looks like it's time to get our money back," she said.

He stood. "High time."

"What's the plan?" she said.

Shepherd turned and grinned. "I was just going to walk in unless you have a better idea."

"Walk in on the 12 Locas biker gang? That ought to be fun to watch."

He laughed.

Gingerly pulling on her thick leather jacket to make sure she didn't hurt her sore arm, Lucky got ready. She pulled on her steel-toe boots and then checked her guns as Shepherd did the same. She stuffed one Glock 45 in her back waistband and a Glock 19 in her shoulder holster. Those biker chicks were not a joke.

As they closed the motel door behind them and headed for the stairs, Lucky rolled her eyes and said, "You're just going to walk in, huh? And with just one gun? They're going to think you're the only one who's loco."

28

The black velvet night was filled with stars above the barren stretch of desert far away from city lights. The sky was clear, which meant the desert air was chilly, and Lucky shivered slightly as Shepherd handed her the binoculars.

They were stretched out on a boulder-strewn hill that looked down on the only structure for miles—the 12 Locas hangout. It looked like an abandoned saloon but at least a dozen motorcycles were parked like dominoes near the front door.

One lone bulb shone down on a woman seated near the door with an AK-47 resting in her lap. She was heavyset and wore chaps and a backward baseball hat. Her short sleeves revealed arms tattooed from knuckle to bicep. Every once in a while she reached beside her chair and retrieved a beer bottle that she held to her lips for a few seconds before placing it back down on the ground. The only other time she moved was to seemingly swat away some pesky insect that occasionally buzzed near her head.

Shepherd stood and handed Lucky his Glock 17.

Taking it, she lifted an eyebrow. "Really? Going in unarmed?"

He nodded. "Best way to get them to trust me."

"Your funeral," she said, and tucked the gun into her waistband.

"I'll be back in a few minutes."

"I'll give you ten and then I'm coming in," Lucky said. "And unlike you, I'll be armed to the teeth."

She patted her side arm holster.

"Give me fifteen," he said.

Instead of answering, she leaned over and set a timer on his watch for thirteen minutes.

Making a face, he started to open his mouth to speak when she cut him off.

"In Italy, thirteen is lucky."

"I'll take your word for it," he said, and started down the hill.

He was about a football field's length away from the door when the biker out front noticed him. Scrambling to her feet, she swore loudly, her chair tipping over behind her.

"Hey!" she shouted. "Don't take another step!"

She aimed the assault rifle at him.

"Easy!" Shepherd shouted. "I'm not armed."

He walked forward with his hands high above his head.

His feet shuffled in the dirt, creating a small dust cloud as he tried to walk slowly.

"Stop right there," the woman said, and took a step back, keeping the assault rifle aimed at his chest. "I'm a dead-eye."

"I believe you," Shepherd said. "I saw you in action today. You took out one of those Aryan Nation morons right between his eyes at two hundred yards with a shotgun. Impressed the hell out of me."

"That was nothing," the woman said. "I was just playing."

"I just want to talk to your boss. I'm not armed and I don't intend to cause any problems. I knew what I was walking up on and I have something important enough to say to her to risk my own neck."

The woman chewed on the side of her lip for a second, head tilted, watching Shepherd.

Then she lowered the gun and, without taking her eyes off Shepherd, reached behind her and flung open the door.

"Yo!" she shouted. "We got company. Possibly a friendly. Can't tell just yet."

Half a dozen bikers filed out and flanked the door, holding guns.

Shepherd was closer now. He had six women pointing weapons at him.

Then, a woman yelled out the open door, "Send him in."

The bodyguard shrugged, stepped aside, and waved her arm in an exaggerated welcome gesture.

"You heard the boss," she said. "Must be your lucky day."

"That's what I was told earlier," he said.

Shepherd had to duck to step inside the crooked doorway.

Inside, a petite woman with black leather pants and a sleeveless T-shirt sat at the bar facing the mirror. Her straight black hair hung in a shiny sheet down her back all the way to her waist. Her left arm sported a large eagle tattoo. The eagle was clutching a snake in its claws. She had a beer bottle with condensation sitting in front of her. The label had been peeled off and was stacked neatly on top of several other similar labels near her right elbow. Her eyes were gray steel and they roamed over Shepherd as she took a swig of her bottle and plopped it loudly on the bar.

She spun on her stool and faced him.

Petra Torres had broad, defined cheekbones and a scar that ran the length of her jaw.

Shepherd took a step toward her. As he did, four women peeled themselves off the walls and pointed their guns at him.

"Whoa! I'm unarmed."

"You're stupid then," another woman sitting at the bar beside Torres said. She had a shaved head, a pierced eyebrow, and a teardrop tattoo near her left eye indicating that she had killed people.

"My friend outside, however, is heavily armed and she's an expert marksman," Shepherd said quickly. "She said I have ten minutes before she storms this place, guns blazing."

"She's stupid, too," the woman with the shaved head said.

Torres gave a slight nod and the other women retreated to their positions along the walls, except for the one with the shaved head, who remained sitting at the bar beside Torres.

After eyeing Shepherd from head to toe, very slowly and without expression, Torres said, "You're partner's a bitch?"

He shrugged. "I don't know if she'd like you calling her that, but yeah, she's a, well, a female, if that's what you're getting at."

Torres nodded. "I saw her at the revival."

"Yeah," Shepherd said.

"Why are you here?"

Shepherd displayed one of his disarming grins. "Saw all the bikes parked out front and thought it would be a good place to grab a cold one."

Trying to hide her smirk, Petra Torres spun her stool back around and nodded at the bartender. He slid a beer in front of the empty seat next to Torres.

Shepherd sat down on the stool and lifted his beer bottle. The woman clinked her bottle against his.

"You've got some big cojones walking into my clubhouse," she said.

"You've got some big ones yourself stealing from Orozco," he responded.

For the first time since he walked in, Torres reacted.

Her steel gray eyes widened and her face grew ashen.

"Listen," Shepherd said, and took another swig of his beer before continuing. "You obviously didn't know it was cartel money. And if you haven't had time to count it yet, I'll tip you off—it's a cool four hundred thousand, which isn't chump change."

A few of the women swore, but Torres remained stone-faced.

"The way I figure it, there's still a way to work this out so nobody dies."

Torres scoffed but didn't say anything.

"I'm serious," Shepherd said.

Torres turned to him and slowly lifted the hem of her shirt. His eyes widened as she pulled it over her head. She was wearing a modest white bra. But that wasn't what she wanted Shepherd to see.

Her chest and abdomen were riddled with jagged, gnarled, deep purple scars.

Shepherd met her eyes.

"Me and my crew," Torres said, shaking her head very slowly, "we aren't afraid of death."

"Everybody fears death," he said as she lowered her shirt. "And unfortunately, this is one situation where you're not going to escape it. The cartel won't stop until they have your head. Nobody wants to live that way—with that hanging over them. Trust me."

Torres took a sip of her beer and then said, "Since, as you put it, we're already dead, then what do you suggest we do, then?"

"Give me the money and then disappear," Shepherd said. "At least then you have a chance."

The women who lined the walls burst into laughter.

Torres said, "If I did that, my own crew would kill me."

"Then your crew isn't as loyal as they should be," he said. "I'll bring back the money and put in a good word for you. I'll say you had no idea it was cartel money and that the second you heard it was, you were eager to return it."

"That makes us sound like cowards," she said, and scowled. "We're not *pinche cobardes*. We are ride or die. If word gets out we ran scared with our tail between our legs from the cartel, we might as well just start a freaking knitting circle."

"Maybe so," he said. "But at this point, it's your only option. Actually, mine, too. This way we both keep our heads a little longer. You've seen what the cartel likes to do with heads to send a message, right? I'm here to warn you that if you don't hand over the money, you're dead and all your family members are dead. I'm your only hope to get out of this alive."

Torres didn't answer. The woman on her other side with the shaved head leaned over. The two of them bowed their heads together and whispered for a few seconds.

Then Torres looked up. "It's just the two of you—you and your bitch?"

Shepherd winced. "You really don't want to call her that, especially to her face."

Torres waved her hand in irritation to dismiss his words.

"Yes, it's just the two of us," Shepherd said, and twisted his wrist to look down at his watch. The movement made the woman with the shaved head freeze and tense up. "You're about two minutes away from meeting her in person. And trust me, you don't want to do that. At least not under these circumstances."

Torres looked at the woman with the shaved head. The other woman immediately slipped off her stool and headed toward another door nearby. A few seconds later, she returned and slid a duffel bag onto the bar in front of Torres.

Opening the bag, Torres fished around and withdrew a stack of cash. Then she pushed the bag toward Shepherd.

He raised an eyebrow at the stack of cash on the bar in front of her.

"For the families of my crew members who were killed today."

The women in the room made soft affirming sounds.

Shepherd gave a solemn nod.

Then he stood and picked up the duffle bag.

"Here's to all of us living another day," he said.

Torres stood as well, and the two faced each other in silence for a second before she said, "We may be a small crew, but we're fierce. We honor our debts. And we owe you. Should the time come, our lives are yours—*una deuda de vida por una deuda de vida.*"

"Hopefully that day never comes," Shepherd said, and walked out.

As he stepped into the night, he glanced down at his watch and saw that the timer had ten seconds left. He looked to the horizon and saw a female silhouette standing tall on the hill. In the light of the moon, he could also see that she was holding a very large weapon at her side. He saw her raise it to her face. It was pointing right at him. In case she could see his face through the scope, he gave an exaggerated wink.

Seconds later, the figure sat back down and her silhouette blended into the terrain.

Exhaling tension he didn't even realize he had, Shepherd headed back up the hill.

29

The desert was bitter cold at night when she was standing still, but on the back of a motorcycle it was bitingly, bone-chillingly so. Lucky buried her face into Shepherd's warmth in front of her on the motorcycle as they roared down the long, flat, deserted highway. She was wearing a thick hoodie under her own leather jacket, but the cold seeped through both layers. She knew Shepherd, on the front of the bike, taking the brunt of the biting wind, must be even colder.

Her hands clutched at the sides of his open motorcycle jacket since she couldn't reach all the way around him. She pressed her face into his leather-clad back, looking off to the side at the star-strewn velvet sky, her hair whipping wildly in the night air.

The rumble of the bike and the warmth of Shepherd's body was relaxing, but Lucky's mind was racing, her thoughts on the duffel bag full of cash strapped to her back. The sooner they got rid of it, the better.

A warm glow lit up the sky a few miles before they reached the small town. Lucky sat up straighter and tensed as they grew closer.

Within moments, Shepherd pulled into a closed gas station. Next door was a small used car lot. Only a dozen vehicles, with prices painted on their windshields, were parked in the lot.

Lucky hopped off first and stretched her legs and arms.

"You going to tell those bikers we're leaving their ride here?" she asked.

"Already a done deal," he said.

They headed next door to the used car lot. Lucky walked in front of the line of vehicles, eyeing them carefully, while Shepherd took the back. They both stopped at the same vehicle—a beat-up Chevy truck.

Lucky shrugged off the straps of the duffle bag and handed it off to Shepherd. Then she headed toward a small office in one corner of the lot. Before she got there, she pulled up her hood and tucked her face inside. A security camera was pointed at the door. Lucky reached into her jacket pocket and extracted a small tool. Within seconds, she made short work of the lock. Once inside, she quickly poked around near the front door, looking for alarm wires, but found nothing. Still, she hurried behind the small desk. The top drawer was locked. After searching for a key and finding nothing, she also picked the lock on the drawer. A jumble of keys were scattered inside. She quickly spotted the one for the Chevy truck. Before leaving, she plucked a wad of cash from an inside pocket and left it on the desk under a large metal paperweight.

Less than ten minutes after they pulled in, Shepherd was in the driver's seat, peeling out of the used car lot as Lucky dialed Dominguez from the passenger seat.

Before he had a chance to speak, Lucky said, "We've got the cash back. Where's the meet?"

Dominguez reeled off the name of an oil drilling site.

"It's ten minutes out of Odessa," he said.

Lucky was looking at the site on her phone's map.

"We'll be there in thirty," she said, and hung up.

Shepherd looked at the map briefly. "We're only about fifteen minutes out."

Lucky smiled. "Coffee," she said. "Maybe you don't need coffee after being awake all night, but I do."

"Good idea," he said. "I remember what you're like in the mornings when you don't have your coffee first."

"I was actually thinking the same damn thing about you," she quipped.

"I'm fine without coffee," he said. "I'm like a ray of sunshine in the morning whether I have coffee or not."

"You keep telling yourself that," Lucky said. "We should probably grab some food while we're at it; you're starting to look a little scrawny."

She reached over and grabbed his arm. "Yeah. Definitely need to fatten you up."

He scoffed and flexed his biceps under her grip. She laughed as the smooth flesh turned to steel.

"We don't have time for food."

"Damn," she said, and sighed. "You're right. I should've told him an hour. Then I could've snuck in a cat nap, too."

"Take your nap now. The map shows a drive-through coffee place five minutes away from the meet."

Refreshed from a ten-minute cat nap and a large cup of coffee, Lucky stretched as they pulled into the driveway of the oil drill site. The sign was rusted and hanging by one bolt. The place was obviously long abandoned.

In the pre-dawn, with the faintest light coming up on the horizon, the mammoth, rusted drilling equipment and platforms looked like prehistoric creatures frozen in time in an oversized graveyard. A large black SUV was parked nearby one of the more intact structures.

Shepherd parked perpendicular to the SUV and waited, his headlights illuminating the other vehicle.

The driver's door opened and Chavez stepped out.

Lucky tensed and balled her hands into fists.

"Fantastic, it's my favorite knucklehead," Shepherd said, and exhaled loudly.

Both men still had visible signs of their encounter in the jail. Shepherd's right eye had a small scab where it was cut. Chavez still sported a black eye, and an angry scar ran down one cheek. He glared at the truck and spat on the ground before hooking his thumbs in his belt loops. His right hand wasn't far from a pistol in his hip holster.

"Aw, he missed you," Lucky said. "Maybe he wants you to give him another black eye so he has a matching set."

"Might as well get this over with." Shepherd slid out of the driver's side door, holding his own gun loosely by his side.

Lucky got out too and then turned to grab the duffle bag. They both stood in front of the truck, the headlight beams casting long shadows in front of them.

Chavez scowled and opened the back door of his SUV without turning around. After he stepped away, Lucky looked at Shepherd, who was gripping his gun. He nodded.

Walking over to the car, Lucky placed the bag in the back seat without taking her eyes off Chavez. Then she walked back to Shepherd.

"What next?" she asked.

"Orozco is pleased," Chavez said. "He'll be in touch. Lie low for a while."

Just then a large black truck with tinted windows pulled up. An Aryan Nation and a Confederate flag flapped in the wind, attached to a pole in the truck bed.

Lucky and Shepherd tensed. The truck pulled up next to Chavez and the window slowly rolled down. A man with a shaved head and tattooed neck nodded, and Chavez handed him the duffle bag through the open window. The window went back up and the truck drove away. Seconds later, Chavez climbed into the SUV and drove away in a small puff of dust.

Lucky shivered involuntarily. Shepherd immediately shrugged off his thick leather jacket and wrapped it around her shoulders. His hands felt hot as they brushed against her neck, sending another shiver down her spine.

"You okay, Lady Luck?"

He was suddenly in front of her, looking down at her face with an expression she couldn't read.

"I'm fine," she said, and spun on her heel.

"Lucky?" he said in a voice she hadn't heard before.

She turned. "What?"

Inwardly, she winced. Her tone came out harsher than she'd intended.

He looked at her for a long moment and then gave a sad smile.

"Nothing."

She turned and hopped in the driver's seat of the truck.

Shepherd had turned away from the truck and stood facing the rising sun, staring at something only he could see.

After a few minutes, he climbed into the passenger seat.

They didn't speak until they were back on the main road.

"Your turn for a nap," Lucky said. "I'll wake you when I find a good place to eat. I could go for some steak and eggs and maybe some Texas toast and more coffee."

"I know just the place," Shepherd said.

"Around here?" Lucky asked in a skeptical tone.

He shrugged. "Maybe an hour from here. Good food. Great coffee. Plus it's a place we can lie low for a bit."

"It better be good," she said. "I'm starving."

"It'll be worth the wait." Shepherd grinned, reached for her phone, and plugged in an address. "Trust me. You won't be disappointed."

30

After she'd been driving for about half an hour, Shepherd had woken up and offered to take over. Lucky hadn't argued. He'd always needed less sleep than she had.

As she drifted off to sleep, Lucky remembered one particular night in a magical Arabian city where they had holed up in a huge loft space high in the sky to recover from a particularly harrowing mission. As the sun had set, a cool breeze had blown long white curtains across the bare floors of the loft, and for once, Shepherd had drifted off to sleep before her.

On that afternoon, Lucky had propped herself on one elbow and examined the man as he slept. She knew him better than anyone and yet she also knew that she didn't know him. Not really. He was an enigma.

Now, during the Texas dawn, Lucky drifted off to sleep thinking she didn't know him any better now, many years later.

She tossed and turned in a restless sleep tormented by images of the innocent she hadn't been able to help or save.

She didn't wake until the truck shuddered to a stop.

"We at the restaurant already?" she asked, and yawned.

As she blinked at the bright morning sunlight streaming through the windshield, it took Lucky a few seconds to focus. When she did, instead of seeing a restaurant, she saw a small white clapboard house. It had a small front porch without any rails. An old swing hung from one end of the porch and a man sat in a rocking chair on the other.

"What the?" she said, and sat up straighter, reaching for her weapon. She shot a glance at Shepherd, who just gave her a grin.

"Time to meet my babysitter."

"That's Red?"

The man stood. He was older, in his late fifties maybe, with tanned, weathered skin. Bright blue eyes under bushy eyebrows squinted at the sun. He ran a hand through his shoulder-length, wavy gray hair and then scratched at his neatly trimmed beard as he stood waiting at the top of the porch steps.

Shepherd leaped out, and to Lucky's amazement, he ran up to the guy and embraced him in a bear hug.

Shaking her head as she got out of the truck, Lucky heard a dog yapping and whining furiously. It took her a few seconds to realize why the sound sent a rush of joy through her. As comprehension dawned, Red reached behind him and opened the screen door to the house.

The Pomeranian came bounding out of the house and leaped, clearing two steps as he raced toward Lucky.

"Chewbacca!" Lucky dropped to the ground, crouching, eyes wide in amazement as she scooped up the dog and scratched his belly. He wriggled wildly and started making gasping sounds like he was choking.

"Who names their dog Chewbacca?" Shepherd made a face.

The man with the blue eyes was off the porch now. "Think the little feller is hyperventilating."

Lucky glanced between him and Shepherd. Both men were grinning at her like maniacs.

"Come on in. I'm just getting ready to make some breakfast," Red said.

After sitting down in the bright, cheery kitchen at the far end of a scratched wooden table, Lucky watched the two men as they talked and joked in front of the stove.

She was absentmindedly scratching the dog's belly when it dawned on her.

"Hey," she said. "You were at the bank."

Red turned and grinned.

Her eyes narrowed. "I knew it. I saw you. You were sitting at the cafe across the street when I pulled up. I recognize you now."

Red laughed. "You got a hell of a memory on you, girl."

"Girl?"

"No offense."

Lucky stared at him for a nanosecond and then said, "None taken."

She scratched the dog's head. "Thanks for taking such good care of Chewie. I think he's even gotten a little fat."

"I've been dribbling bacon drippings on his dog food. He was too skinny."

"Fact," she said. "He found me after I moved to Juarez. He was wandering the streets in my neighborhood and looked like he hadn't eaten for days."

"Those mutts go for four thousand or something, right? I can't imagine someone would abandon him."

"They abandoned the entire neighborhood during the cartel wars," Lucky said.

"That's true. Poor feller probably accidentally got left behind."

"Well thanks for grabbing him."

"Yup," Red said, and slid a plate of bacon, eggs, and cheese grits in front of her. The three sat down to dig in.

Lucky broke off bits of her bacon to feed the dog.

After they'd cleaned their plates, Lucky sat back and examined Red.

"Now who exactly are you, Red?" she said. "I mean I know you are this guy's handler, but you seem like more than that. As far as I knew, this big lunk didn't have any friends."

Red laughed. "He doesn't. Not really. I'm the only one who can put up with his lone wolf act. I see right through that. That stuff doesn't fly with me."

Shepherd looked down, neck reddening.

Lucky laughed loudly. "I don't know if I've ever seen him embarrassed before. Holy smokes!"

"Not embarrassed," Shepherd said.

"Ha! Are too!" Red chimed in.

"Am not."

Red looked back and forth between the two of them with a huge grin. Finally he grew serious.

"I met Shepherd at the lowest point of my life. He put me in touch with Max. Because of my unique skillset, The Foundation decided I would be the one assigning Shepherd to ops."

"What are your unique skills?" Lucky asked.

"It's a long, boring story, but I used to oversee some major covert military operations."

Shepherd gave a fake cough that sounded like "bin Laden."

"Did you say bin Laden?" Lucky asked, her eyes wide.

"Didn't say nothing," Shepherd said.

"Yeah," Red added. "He just coughed."

Lucky rolled her eyes. "That's all I get?" she asked.

"For now." Red winked.

"Here's what's been going on since I saw you in Juarez," Shepherd said, and then filled Red in. As he laid out the details of the previous few days, Red's eyebrows knit together. Finally, when he was done, Shepherd sat back.

"I don't like it," Red said.

"Same," Lucky said.

"I wouldn't trust any of them, not a one." Red looked at Shepherd.

"That's why we have to go after them right now," Lucky said.

Then Shepherd looked at Red and raised his eyebrow. "You know what we need."

"She's not ready yet," Red answered.

This time Lucky looked from one man's face to the other.

"The hell I'm not," she said, and stood. "I was born ready."

Red laughed. "I believe that. We weren't talking about you. We're talking about the Hate Truck."

Lucky lifted an eyebrow. "The hate what? Truck? What?"

"The Hate Truck," Shepherd affirmed.

"No clue what that is."

"You're going to have to see for yourself." Red scraped back his chair and stood. "Come on now. She's in the barn."

He led them out the back door and toward the barn at the rear of the property.

Once there, Shepherd threw open the large doors.

The front end of a semi-trailer faced them. Instead of a normal hood, six large metal plates formed a star with a pylon-shaped metal rod at the end that stuck out from the cab. The addition effectively made the entire vehicle a massive battering ram. Mounted on top of the semi-truck cab was a semicircle of thick metal with a heavy artillery mount behind it.

"So this is the Hate Truck?" She let out a low whistle. "What's the story behind the name?"

"You take all the hate inside you and pour it into that truck so you can unleash hell when the time comes," Shepherd said.

Red climbed up to demonstrate how he could man the .50 caliber machine gun on the mount and still be protected by the thick semi-circle of metal that shielded him up to his armpits.

After climbing a small set of steps leading up to the flatbed of the cab, Lucky gestured toward an area marked with spray paint. "What goes here?"

"A custom box that will hold other weapons. They'll be clipped in so they can be retrieved easily. The box won't have a lid so whoever is back here can reach inside and grab anything they need—a rifle, a grenade, a rocket launcher."

A few other mounts lay on the truck bed.

"These need to be welded on still," Shepherd said.

Lucky nodded her approval.

"Nice, but why didn't you just buy a decommissioned Bearcat or something?"

"What fun is that?" Shepherd said.

"Um, maybe not fun, but easy."

"You obviously aren't a car guy," Red said with a big wink. "I grew up fixing cars with my dad. It's a lot more fun than it looks."

Lucky hopped off the back of the truck and headed for a nearby workbench. She grabbed a welding mask and then tossed one to Shepherd.

"Let's do this," she said. "I need some fun in my life."

Shepherd turned to Red.

"I need a fifty."

Red pulled a chain on the floor. A trap door lifted and a set of stairs led down to a well-lit room. Even from the top of the stairs, it was clear that the underground room contained a fully stocked armory. The walls were lined with every sort of weapon imaginable, from daggers to broad swords, from tiny pistols to rocket launchers.

"I think you'll find everything you need down here," Red said as he and Shepherd climbed down and started retrieving weapons.

Lucky peered down at the two men and grinned.

"Red, I have a feeling you and I are going to get along just fine."

31

The sky to the west had turned a deep red shot with pink when Red opened the barn door.

"I'll let you two finish up while I feed the horses and get dinner started," he said.

They watched Red leave. Lucky had a black smudge of grease on her cheek and dust in her hair. Shepherd's arms were covered in grease up to his elbows.

"He's good people," she said.

"The best," Shepherd answered.

He turned toward Lucky. She was absentmindedly rubbing her arm.

"Arm still sore?"

"It's fine," Lucky said dismissively.

Shepherd yawned and she followed suit, lifting her arms above her head in a long, feline-like stretch. As she did, her shirt rode up and revealed the taut skin of her abdomen.

Despite himself, Shepherd stared at the bare flesh.

Lucky noticed immediately. She lowered her arms and waited for his gaze to travel up to her face. When it did, they locked eyes for a second and then he looked away.

She turned toward the truck and began to arrange a set of knives along a makeshift tool belt-like structure just under the back window.

A few seconds later, she hopped off the truck bed at the same moment Shepherd turned around, and they crashed into one another.

He grabbed her waist to help her regain her balance.

"Sorry," he said, and turned away. Before he could take a step, she leaped on him and slammed him into the side of the truck.

It was a tense, fierce, tender moment with their bodies pressed together tightly. Lucky had her hands on Shepherd's forearms, pinning him against the door. Her neck was arched and her head tilted back, eyes ablaze as she glared at his lips.

Shepherd's head was bowed toward hers and his eyelids were half-closed.

A primal urge that had been building since that day in the bank was now barreling full speed. They were caught up in a tsunami of deep-seated emotions that made common lust feel like child's play.

The instant their bodies pressed together, there was no turning back.

Bodies arched.

Grease-stained hands and fingers roamed across silky skin.

Beefy hands gripped her buttocks, lifting her up as her legs snaked around his waist.

Her arms wrapped around his neck, mouths glued together, as he carried her to the bed of the truck.

One violent swoop sent an assortment of tools, guns, and metal sheets off the truck bed and crashing onto the floor. She was on her back under him and he propped himself up on his hands so he didn't crush her.

A second later, she used her thighs to flip him over so his back was pressed down on the cold metal of the truck bed. She straddled him and ripped off her shirt, tossing it behind her.

Reaching down, she undid his shirt. He watched her, the look in his eyes something she'd never seen before. It sent a thrill through her, an unfamiliar mixture of danger, excitement, and fear.

Quickly she looked away and stood, shrugging out of her cargo pants as he wriggled to shed his own.

Then, with a small snarl, she was astride him. Both gasped as they became one and rocked almost violently against one another, exploring familiar territory that felt both like home and a lifetime ago.

When she realized that tears had slipped out of her eyes, she angrily brushed them away.

He reached up and tried to wipe away a few stray tears, but she swatted his hand away and leaned down to bite him. Just a little. Just a warning. But she still left small, perfect tooth marks on his upper chest.

His fingers were tangled in her hair, pulling her toward him, kissing every bit of her flesh his mouth could reach.

His eyes remained glued to her face. She looked away for a few seconds, but when she glanced back, he was still looking at her so intensely that she closed her eyes to escape. She reared her head back and lost herself completely and with utter abandon.

It had been a hell of a long time, but she was finally back home.

If only for a few moments in time.

When Lucky and Shepherd finally emerged from the barn, the sun had set.

Their faces were flushed. Shepherd's grease-stained shirt was buttoned up, but the buttons were askew.

Across the yard, the windows of the house were lit up, and a string of lights hanging under the eaves on the front porch created a party atmosphere.

They walked side by side, silent.

Red was sitting on the porch swing with a glass of something iced. A pitcher rested on a table nearby. He glanced at them, one bushy eyebrow rising imperceptibly, but his face remained neutral.

"Good timing," Red said. "I just took the roast out of the oven. You have time to go get cleaned up while it rests."

"I think I'm in heaven," Shepherd said, and inhaled deeply.

Red slowly looked from Shepherd to Lucky. "Truer words were never spoken."

Lucky felt a flush crawl up her neck and swallowed her discomfort.

Seeing this, Red quickly quipped, "Hope you aren't a vegan or something, Lucky."

The tension was broken.

She scoffed. "Hardly."

"Good." He winked. "There's towels and soap and all that in the bathroom off the kitchen for you, Adam. Lucky, go on upstairs and help yourself to the master bath. You'll find everything you need there. I even have some clean clothes that might fit you. I put some out on the bed."

As soon as they stepped inside and the door closed behind them, Shepherd turned to Lucky. She froze, eyes wide, half afraid of what was going to come out of his mouth. He reached over and gently ran the back of his hand across her clavicle just below her neck.

"Where's your necklace, Lucia."

Her breath caught in her throat. It was the second time he'd asked and the first time he'd ever called her by her real name. This time she would answer. It was his tone. She quickly blew out a big puff of air and the moment was gone.

"Mrs. Orozco," she said, and shook her head. "She wanted it. It was before the Guzman deal."

Shepherd's eyes narrowed dangerously. "You gave it to her?"

Lucky shrugged. "I had to prove myself to them."

"I'm gonna get it back for you," he said fiercely.

She turned and walked away before he could say anything else.

After her shower, Lucky found three flowered dresses laid out neatly on the bed. A lump rose in her throat when she realized what they were. She fingered one softly and then held it up to her. She walked over to the large dresser covered with photos of Red and a blonde woman. They were young and laughing in every photo.

One small silver frame held a memorial prayer card from the woman's funeral service.

Lucky swallowed. It felt like something was stuck in her throat. Across the room, in an open closet, she could see other dresses hanging.

After an internal debate about the significance of wearing Red's dead wife's clothes, Lucky decided it was an honor and slipped on the plainest dress he set out—a faded red one with small white flowers.

Nervously, she walked into the kitchen.

Red beamed at her, his bright blue eyes twinkling. "That one was Mary's favorite. I just knew you were going to pick it."

"It's lovely. I saw the pictures of you and your wife. She's so beautiful."

Red nodded, still grinning. "She was my everything."

"Are you sure it's okay for me to wear this?" Lucky asked.

"It's more than okay. Mary would have loved you," he said. "She would be pleased as punch to have you wear her clothing. If she were here right now, she would have insisted the same as I am."

"Okay," Lucky said, and smiled. "Then it's my honor."

The three of them devoured the roast, potatoes, and gravy in minutes.

After they cleared the table and tackled the dishes as a team, Shepherd reached for his leather jacket.

"I'm going to head into town to talk to Dusty," he said, and turned to Lucky. "He's the American Fast Eddie."

"Aha," she said.

"If there's anything going on with Orozco, he'll know," Shepherd said.

Red reached for the wine bottle. "Good. It'll give me and Lucky some time to get to know each other better."

"I'd like that," she said.

***

The older man behind the counter at the general store nervously eyed Shepherd as he wandered the aisles, picking up a bottle of juice here or examining a package of cookies there. Shepherd was trying to appear both unthreatening and inconspicuous, but a sumo wrestler trying to blend into a little girl's ballerina class would have had more luck.

Finally, the front door chimed as a man entered the store wearing a Hawaiian shirt with long, stringy blond hair under a straw cowboy hat.

He eyed Shepherd and they both headed toward the refrigerated section that housed the beer.

"Hear anything?" Shepherd said immediately.

Looking over his shoulder, the cowboy began to speak quickly.

"You know Orozco has a safe house in Candelaria right near the border of Mexico, right?"

"Yeah?"

"After your text, I decided to drive by there on my way here," he said. "And wouldn't you know it, I saw something."

Shepherd tensed as Dusty continued.

"There was a crew leaving from the safe house. I followed them until they turned off at Hot Springs Road. I got here as fast as I could."

Shepherd hurriedly stuffed a wad of bills into Dusty's shirt pocket and raced out, the door slamming loudly behind him.

Red lived off of Hot Springs Road.

32

Lucky's belly was warm from the red wine she and Red were sipping as they sat at the large wooden table. She was a little sleepy and happy and sore, the way she liked to feel after a hard day's work.

"I'm glad Shepherd has you in his corner," Red said. "He doesn't open up to very many people. But I can tell he really trusts you."

For some reason she didn't understand, Lucky blushed. She raised her wine glass and took a sip to hide it.

Setting her glass back down, she said, "Tell me how you two met."

"You're real good at changing the subject." Red winked.

"How long have you guys known each other?"

"A few years after Kabul," he said pointedly, stroking his neatly trimmed gray beard. He ran his hand over his long, wavy gray hair and gave a knowing smile.

She nodded slowly as she found herself suddenly lost in memories.

Red cleared his throat and she snapped back.

"I met him in a bar outside Juarez," he said.

"Of course you did." Lucky laughed.

"I was living off the grid after Mary passed. I just wanted to be drunk and not think. I also wanted to fight anything that moved. So I was there starting shit," he said. "I probably was looking for an easy way out of my pain. These guys were low-level drug runners for the cartel. Pretty much hot-headed nobodies who wouldn't be missed but who were still trying to prove themselves. In other words, they were dangerous."

"Sounds like it," Lucky said.

Red's voice was low, deep, soothing, and mesmerizing. She ran a finger around the rim of her wine glass absentmindedly as she listened.

"Anyway, I can't remember what I said or did, but I was looking for trouble and I found it. They were on me, beating the living daylights out of me. It was five to one. The bartender was the only one there and he flat-out left, headed for the hills.

"They had me on the ground and then one of them was on top of me and holding a blade to my throat. And wouldn't you know, right then and there I decided that I didn't actually want to die despite what I'd been telling myself since Mary's death. But at that point it was too late. Or so I thought."

He paused dramatically.

Lucky raised an eyebrow and he continued.

"Then the guy on me was suddenly gone. And the rest of them were gone, too. I heard all sorts of sounds but it was pretty hard to see because they'd beaten me so badly my eyes were practically swollen shut. I scooted back against the wall and used my fingers to prop open my eyelid on one eye. There was Shepherd, standing near the door. The five losers were all on the ground moaning. Shepherd came over and offered me his hand. I owe him my life."

The two sat in silence for a few seconds, each lost in their own thoughts.

The wooden table was scratched and worn yet polished and smooth. Running her hands across it, Lucky felt a nostalgia she had no reason to experience. The well-loved piece of furniture had clearly witnessed a life well lived. Family dinners. Late-night glasses of wine. Boisterous card games.

Maybe even some hanky-panky. Her eyes widened at the thought that had come out of nowhere.

She looked up to find Red watching her.

"So I owe him my life. Probably a couple times over," Red said.

"Nah." Lucky took a sip of her wine.

"Hell yes I do."

She shook her head again, a teasing smile on her face.

"Then what the heck would you call it?" Red scratched his head. "He saved my life. I owe him a life debt. That's how I see it."

"I don't know about life debts," Lucky said. "But I do know about vendettas. My mother was Italian."

"I thought you were Mexican?" he said.

"Half. My parents met on a Doctors Without Borders mission in El Salvador. My mother was a doctor, my father was a volunteer. They traded it for life on a farm."

Red's eyebrows knit together. "This farm? Does it have something to do with your vendetta?"

"You know." It was a statement, not a question.

Looking sheepish, Red nodded. "Shepherd told me. The Orozco Cartel killed your dad when he refused to hand over his farm."

Looking down, Lucky didn't answer.

"Why don't I get us some more wine," he said, and stood.

"No more for me," Lucky said. "I'm working."

"You call this work?" he asked.

"I allow myself more than one glass if I'm totally off the grid somewhere living in a hut on a deserted stretch of beach where the only threat is maybe a little tropical rain cutting my beach day short."

"So you're always alert for danger?" Red tilted his head.

"Aren't you?" she replied archly.

He nodded. "Damn right I am."

"Tell me about Mary," she said impulsively, thinking about the table. "How did she die?"

He stared at Lucky for a long moment and then said, "During childbirth. I lost them both."

"I'm so sorry."

She put her hand on his and squeezed.

After he left the military, Red bought a farm and decided he wanted nothing more than to live off the grid, raise chickens and cattle and a bevy of kids with a loving wife. He'd known from the second he set eyes on Mary that she was the one for him. They'd met at the county fair one summer. She was a college girl from the city visiting friends.

They fell in love and got married as soon as Mary graduated from college, eager to start a family.

Mary started her accounting business working out of the farmhouse, helping the neighboring farmers with taxes and keeping their books. She kept working right up until hours before she was taken to the hospital in labor.

"Never for one second when they whisked her in to do an emergency C-section did I think she wouldn't come back out of there." He looked off in the distance and swiped at his eyes.

"I'm so sorry," Lucky said again.

"She would've loved you," he said. "You'd have been fast friends."

"Thank you." Lucky looked down at a deep groove in the worn wood and traced it lightly with one finger.

After a moment, Lucky asked, "You talked about a special skillset. Was that from when you were in the military?"

He met her eyes and slowly nodded.

Then he cleared his throat and said, "It's a long story for another time."

They sat there in comfortable silence for a few seconds. Then his eyes narrowed and he quickly stood. Lucky did too, alarm zinging through her limbs.

They both had heard it at once: the low growl of an army of vehicles descending on the farm. They were on their feet in seconds.

Without a word, Red pivoted and opened a long cupboard door. A shotgun and several pistols hung from hooks on the inside. He tossed Lucky a handgun, stuffed one in the back of his jeans, and grabbed the shotgun.

They ran into the front room. Through a long window pane flanking the front door, Lucky could see three large SUVs already stopped in front of the house.

Red motioned for Lucky to stay near the kitchen door. She crouched against the doorjamb, making her the smallest target possible.

Keeping to the wall, Red made his way to a window beside the door.

Using a large dresser to shield his body, he pulled aside a sliver of the curtain.

The movement was met with a flurry of gunfire that ripped through the walls of the farmhouse above the dresser, shattering several of the framed pictures set on top of it.

Red ducked and made his way back to the kitchen by hugging the far wall.

Several blasts took out the glass panes flanking the side of the door.

Lucky was now standing toward the rear of the kitchen. She had her legs spread and her gun held in both hands in front of her, facing the front door.

Then Lucky saw something through a broken pane of glass.

A man with a small, eyeless skull tattooed between his eyebrows.

It was that bastard Chavez. She swore softly.

He was marching steadily forward, unloading a shotgun that was splintering the thick front door.

"We're outnumbered," Red said. He stood and ran for the back door. "We've got to get to the Hate Truck."

He held the door open for Lucky and yelled, "Go! Go! Go!"

Without looking back, Lucky sprinted out the door. Behind her she heard the front door shatter and more windows breaking. At first, Red was right on her heels. She could hear his panting breath as he ran. The strip of land between the house and barn was open and exposed.

A large light post illuminated their way.

Chavez and his men bolted through the house while a few others ran alongside it. A volley of gunfire peppered the dirt around their feet, and Lucky instinctively zigzagged to dodge the bullets.

She heard a grunt and knew that one round had found its mark. She turned to see Red go down hard, face first in the dirt. He lifted his head and shouted, "Run!"

She ignored him and whirled. She reached down, grabbed his arm, and began to run backward, dragging him toward the barn with one hand and firing with the other.

Then her bullets ran out. The barn was still several feet away.

Suddenly, the gunfire stopped.

Chavez stepped into the light from the shadows of the house.

"Just tell us where the big guy is and we'll let you walk out of here," he shouted.

"Bite me," Red said.

But Lucky hesitated. "How do we know you're telling the truth?" she asked.

The men lowered their weapons and Chavez took a step toward her.

"Just a few steps more," Red said under his breath.

He pulled himself to a standing position, holding onto her arm for balance.

Lucky saw he was reaching behind him for the gun in his waistband.

"You sure about this?" she whispered.

"As soon as I fire, you run for the barn. I'll meet you there at the Hate Truck."

"I don't know," she said. Her finger twitched. She could kill Chavez right now. But he would probably kill Red in return. She couldn't take that chance.

"Do it," he said.

She was going to tell Red to run, but before she could, he stepped in front of her and fired at Chavez.

"Run!" he shouted.

"Damn it," she shouted, and then she turned and ran with everything she was worth as a flurry of bullets pursued her. She dove into the open barn door and tucked and rolled until she was out of range. When she sat up, she realized that Red was not behind her.

"*Cavolo!*" she swore in Italian.

She plucked a gun from the Hate Truck as she passed and, leading with the weapon, ran to the barn door.

What she saw made her stop dead in her tracks.

Chavez was standing over Red's body, pointing a gun at him.

"Last chance, *chica*," he yelled. "You come with me or the old man dies."

He fired his gun and Lucky screamed and jumped. The bullet had gone into Red's leg.

"That was my only warning," Chavez said.

"Let him go," Lucky shouted, and stepped into the light outside the barn with her hands held high. Her entire body was shaking. She'd dropped the gun in the barn. "Take me!"

"No!" Red's voice broke as he yelled.

Chavez kicked him in the ribs and Red groaned loudly.

"Bring her to me," Chavez said.

Two men ran out of the shadows and grabbed Lucky's arms, yanking them down and then marching her past Red.

She glanced down. The wound to his leg wasn't bleeding too bad. He most likely wouldn't bleed out. Most likely.

Chavez was walking in front of her. He stopped as one of the SUVs pulled around the side of the house. He turned to face Lucky.

"I like you much better in a dress," he said. He took a knife from a holster on his hip and sliced through the top three buttons on the dress. "Much better."

Lucky didn't react. She kept her gaze on his left ear, refusing to meet his eyes.

"If I hadn't been told to bring you back all in one piece I would make you my plaything," he said.

His eyes narrowed as she continued to ignore him.

"Get in." He shoved her toward the SUV's backseat.

She climbed in. Another cartel member—a guy in a cowboy-cut shirt and aviator sunglasses—was already there, leaning against the opposite door and pointing a large gun at her.

Her door was slammed shut. Chavez hopped into the front passenger seat. Lucky briefly considered trying to strangle the driver, but realized she'd be dead before she reached for the man's neck. And the driver wasn't her target. The man in the front passenger seat was. She had already waited years, she could bide her time a little bit longer.

After the driver had started the engine and they were pulling away, she was relieved to see the other cartel members walking away from Red.

But he wasn't moving, and fear ripped through her.

Then one of the cartel members turned and fired at Red. She saw his body bounce from the impact and then he didn't move again.

Lucky screamed and began to tear at the door handle, which wouldn't budge. She turned in her seat, furious and frantic and terrified, and banged on the window, trying to get free, trying to get to Red.

Only when she felt the cold steel on her temple did she settle down.

She faced the front again, rage bubbling up inside her. Chavez had turned around in his seat, facing her.

"You bastard. You killed him anyway." Her voice was filled with venom. "You will pay for this. I promise you."

"Where is he? The big guy?" Chavez pointed a handgun at her, resting it on the seat back. "Tell me and maybe I won't kill you, too."

She pressed her lips together, fury in her eyes.

The man beside her yanked her arms behind her back and bound them.

"Last chance," Chavez said, and tapped the gun.

Very slowly, she shook her head.

"You're going to have to shoot me," she spat out.

The man beside her looped a strip of cloth around her head. She assumed it was to strangle her but he fashioned a gag out of it. She was still glaring at Chavez when a bag was pulled down over her head, engulfing her in blackness.

33

Urging the old pickup truck past one hundred mph, Shepherd leaned forward, white knuckles gripping the steering wheel as he raced toward Red's house. He was swearing and sweating and felt like he was going to vomit.

"Come on!" he yelled, pounding the steering wheel.

He'd tried to call both Lucky and Red what seemed like a million times and neither one had answered. In a rage, he'd thrown his phone across the cab. It had bounced off the window with a cracking sound and now lay on the passenger seat floor, completely out of his reach.

From a mile away he saw the sky light up in an eerie orange glow and his heart sank. As he grew closer, even from the main road, he could see the old farmhouse was ablaze. He turned down the driveway and was met with the sight of huge plumes of black billowing smoke rising from tall flames protruding from the top of the house.

He skidded to a stop in front of the inferno, his tires kicking up dirt and rocks and a huge fishtail of dust. Jumping out of his truck, he could feel the fire's heat as it licked at the farmhouse walls. A searing red and orange cloud had formed above the house.

As he was running toward the front door, the second floor crumbled in an awesome roar and shudder, collapsing onto the main level and leaving a pile of rubble in its wake.

It was too late for anyone who might have been inside.

That was when Shepherd noticed all the tire tracks leading toward the barn.

Darting to the back of the house, he saw a patch of blood on the dirt between the house and the barn. A trail of blood led away from the patch as if somebody had been dragged. Terror and rage spiked through him as he followed the bloody trail at a run, his heart in his throat.

It led around the far side of the barn.

As he rounded the corner, Shepherd saw what at first looked like a clump of clothing. As he grew closer, he saw that a man was lying face down beside a wooden cross at the foot of a large live oak tree.

Red.

Shepherd bolted toward his friend and then knelt, leaning over to check for a pulse.

As he did, Red coughed and wheezed and turned his head to spit blood into the dirt.

His face was covered in dirt.

"I tried to stop them," he said, his voice husky and weak and filled with regret. "But they took her. Lucky."

He gasped the last word.

Shepherd gently rolled him over.

"Let's take a look at what we got going on here."

He kept his voice calm and reassuring even though his hands were shaking.

Red looked up at Shepherd. "I'm in pretty bad shape."

Shepherd's eyes grew slightly wider as he saw the bloody mess he'd turned over.

Red didn't miss any of it.

"I knew it," he said. "That's why I came over here. I wanted to be with Mary when I went."

"You're not going anywhere."

"How bad is it?"

"I've seen worse," Shepherd said.

The majority of the blood loss seemed to be coming from two gunshot wounds to Red's leg. His shirt was also dark with blood at the shoulder, but he didn't seem to be actively bleeding.

Shepherd turned his attention to the leg first.

One of the bullets appeared to have pierced the flesh of Red's thigh and exited the other side. But the other wound didn't look great and the bullet had no exit wound.

The bullet obviously hadn't struck an artery or Red would already be dead. But he was losing a lot of blood. His pant leg was slightly shredded and wet with blood. Shepherd quickly ripped off his own button-down shirt and then tugged off the T-shirt he was wearing underneath. Balling the soft cotton material into a fist, he put it on Red's thigh.

He held it down tight by pressing both palms and leaning his weight onto it. After a few seconds, he lifted the shirt and took a look.

When he did, the blood began to seep again.

This time he pressed his knee on the ball of fabric to maintain pressure and quickly stripped his belt from his pants. He looped the belt under Red and tightened it at the thigh above the wound.

"I don't want a tourniquet. That's how people lose their legs," Red said in a weak voice.

"Nah, that's only if you have it on too long. You'll be fine," Shepherd said. "The medics will be here soon and take off the tourniquet. I just need to keep you from bleeding out until they get here."

"They also got my shoulder," Red offered. "But I think it's a flesh wound. They were in too big a hurry to torch my place and get out of here. Or else they were a shitty shot."

"Shitty shot," Shepherd quipped with a grin.

He tore off Red's shirt to see the shoulder wound. It was bleeding worse than he thought. He was out of fabric now.

Shepherd looked around. If he could just find some type of material to use as a bandage, he could stop the bleeding until help arrived.

He looked down. Red was wearing slip-on Adidas sandals with clean white socks that practically glowed in the dim light. Shepherd reached down, slipped off a sandal, and then pulled off a sock.

"Seriously?"

"Damn right." Shepherd wadded up the sock. "Let's get your shoulder wound elevated."

He scooted Red closer to the wooden cross and lifted him to a sitting position. Then he pushed the balled sock onto the shoulder wound.

"I'm going to need you to hold tight to this sock. Keep pressure on it. Think you can do that?"

"Yeah," Red scoffed. "You think I'm a pansy?"

But his voice was weak.

Shepherd took out his cell phone, punched in some numbers, and said, "We got a gunshot victim at the old Danbury ranch. Get someone out here asap."

He put the phone on Red's lap.

"I've done what I can but a doctor is going to have to get those bullets out."

"I'm not dying in a hospital by myself!" Red said, struggling to get up.

Shepherd put his hand on his shoulder. "Stay put. I don't want the bleeding to get any worse. Besides, you're not going to die. It's not your time yet. Mary's going to have to wait a little longer."

"How do you know?" Red said. "Show me your medical degree, smartass."

Shepherd shot a glance at the cross. "No offense, Mary, but I'm going to be selfish and keep Red with me a little longer."

Red let out a strangled laugh. "You're crazy. I never argued with that woman one day in my life. I'm no dummy. I know what's good for me."

"I'm not arguing. I'm just giving her an update." Shepherd stood.

"Wish you could've met her," Red said.

"Yeah, me too."

"When are you going to settle down with a good woman?"

"Never," Shepherd said.

"Why?"

Shepherd didn't answer, just squinted and looked off in the distance.

"It wouldn't kill you to open up a little, you know?"

"How do you know it won't kill me?" Shepherd grinned. "Show me *your* medical degree."

"Haha," Red said. "I don't feel so great."

Sirens filled the air. It sounded like they were still far away.

"Here they come," Shepherd said. "You'll be in good hands. I've done all I can."

He started to walk toward the barn.

"You going to get Lucky?" Red asked.

Shepherd spoke without turning around.

"Yep. And I'm gonna bring the hate."

34

Through the thin fabric of the hood over her head, Lucky could see the long stretch of black road lit up by the vehicle's headlights as they drove. She could barely make out the dashboard's glowing, blurry green lights. Once, when she leaned forward to see if the dash showed an electronic map or the road they were on, she got a punch in the gut with the nose of a gun.

She sat back and let her head loll to the side, pretending to sleep.

But her mind was racing.

They wanted her alive.

There was a good chance that when they got where they were going, that would all change. They wanted to know where Shepherd was. She knew that she would either be tortured until she told them or used as bait to lure him to them.

Either way, she was merely a tool to get to him.

That meant she was expendable.

She needed to forge a plan to escape while she still could.

At one point she heard soft snoring beside her. Slowly, she turned so her bound hands were facing the door. Through the hood she could make out a dark silhouette in the other seat. Keeping her eyes glued on the gunman for any movement, she snaked her hands toward the door handle, feeling around until her fingers clenched down on it. She wasn't sure what she was going to do when she got the door open—fall backward to her death on the road? She would wait until the vehicle slowed down and then open it.

Then her chance came. The vehicle began to slow. As it did, the man beside her made a soft grunting sound as if he was awakening.

She couldn't wait any longer. She gripped the handle and pulled down.

It didn't budge. The child locks were on.

Damn it.

She was tempted to throw herself at the man sitting beside her but didn't because she was afraid he would just pull the trigger and shoot her.

Chavez and the driver were silent. Every once in a while, one of them said something quietly in Spanish that Lucky couldn't hear over the soft strains of narcocorrido music coming from the vehicle's speakers.

Every bump in the road sent Lucky bouncing up in her seat toward the ceiling.

She used the motion to try to loosen the material binding her wrists. She'd found a tiny tear in the fabric they used to tie her wrists together. When they hit a bump she would use the movement to exclaim loudly so her voice would hide the sound of the fabric ripping.

Then a phone rang. She froze. The man beside her made a snuffling sound and shifted in his seat.

"We got the bitch," Chavez said. "She was hiding out with an old rancher. No sign of the big guy and she's not talking. We'll convince her at the compound."

Then the call ended.

A while later, the vehicle slowed down nearly to a stop. After a wide turn that sent Lucky careening into the door, she heard a gate creak open and the vehicle start up again, this time bumping along a rough road.

She froze now when she saw something in front of her. Through the hood, she could make out a large structure lit up like daylight. The vehicle slowed while a second gate swung open.

The vehicle slammed to a stop and she rocketed toward the front seat, hitting her mouth on the seatback in front of her. She cried out but the gag muffled her sound.

Her door creaked open and she was yanked out of the vehicle. She stumbled but someone grabbed her arms and righted her. Then pushed her.

"Vamos."

She walked toward a large sliding metal door.

It opened as they grew closer.

Two men stood just inside the doorway, holding assault rifles and looking around for any danger.

A gun at her spine prodded her through the door and down a hall that opened into a large room. As she entered the room, the hood was yanked off her head.

She was in a room with a low ceiling and concrete walls. A lightbulb hung from a long cord above a metal chair. A camera on a tripod faced the chair. Plastic sheeting was spread on the ground beneath the chair in a sloppy semi-circle. Her heart leaped into her throat. This was a death trap.

They were going to torture her and kill her and let the plastic collect her body fluids before they wrapped her body in it.

Her only hope was to get her hands free. She tugged at the fabric that had already ripped.

But then the man guarding her whirled her around, and with a swift slice of his knife, her hands were free. She rubbed them together. For some reason, she was now more worried than ever.

"Sit," Chavez ordered. She complied.

The man guarding her the entire trip untied her gag, and she was about to protest when he shoved the muzzle of his gun into her mouth. Meanwhile, Chavez crouched on the plastic, holding a roll of duct tape. He ripped off long, thin strips of the tape. One by one, he taped her fingers to the chair.

"This is going to be fun." He grinned at her, flashing gold teeth.

The guard removed his gun from her mouth and walked out the door. Lucky watched to see if the door locked behind him but couldn't tell.

"Do you remember my father?" Lucky said, arching an eyebrow.

"What?" Chavez was taken off guard. His face scrunched up, making the eyeless skull between his eyebrows crinkle.

"His name was Benito Luis Rodriguez."

"That name means nothing."

Lucky leaned forward. "You don't remember, do you?" she hissed. "That's okay. Because I promise you that his name will be the last thing you hear on this earth."

Chavez laughed. "You talk so big for such a little girl. Once we begin to cut off your fingers, this tough talk will end. And you will tell us where the big guy is."

Lucky glared at him.

"The last thing you will hear—Benito Luis Rodriguez," she said, biting out the words one by one.

Instead of responding, Chavez took a long knife out of a holder. He placed the blade at her neck and then lightly drew it down to the soft indent at her throat.

"Mr. Orozco has some questions for you. I think you'll find it in your best interest to answer him right away. The longer it takes for him to find out what he wants to know, the more fun I get to have." He shrugged. "It's entirely up to you. If you take your time answering, it is ultimately better for me."

Lucky glared at him, her lips pressed tightly together.

"I will do you a small kindness, though, by telling you what the future holds and why it is useless to resist. Because no matter what, you will die. It's just a question of how you die that really matters."

"It doesn't matter what you do, I'm not talking," she said. "Then your boss will see what an inept moron you are. If you can't torture a 'little girl' into giving up a name, then there's a good chance your career as a heavy is over, *amigo*."

Chavez chewed on his lip for a second. She watched the rage grow. Then he walked over and slapped her head so hard, the chair she was on nearly toppled.

After the chair regained its balance, settling back on four legs, Lucky tossed her hair out of her face by shaking her head. She spat blood out of her mouth and glared at him.

"His name was Benito Luis Rodriguez," she gritted out.

35

The concrete-walled room could have easily been an ISIS execution room, Lucky thought, her mind racing through any possible escape options.

Once Chavez got to work, fighting back would become more and more difficult.

Chavez walked over to the small table and began to examine an assortment of weapons arranged neatly on a cloth. Lucky knew what those were used for and swallowed the fear threatening to rise into her throat. The table also contained a computer monitor displaying views from four security cameras. There was a view of the driveway and interior rooms.

While he was occupied, Lucky quickly scanned the small room for weapons or a way to escape. There were no windows, and the door was the only way in or out. The concrete walls were bare.

Lucky wriggled her fingers, trying to loosen the duct tape securing them to the arm of the chair. Unfortunately, Chavez had done a good job.

There was movement on one of the security screens and seconds later the door opened.

Orozco strode into the room, followed by Dominguez.

Wearing an obviously expensive three-piece navy pinstripe suit that was several sizes too large, Orozco cut a comical figure. His round face was sweaty and his full head of hair looked slightly greasy.

Dominguez strode in, his well-worn cowboy boots clicking on the concrete floor, his lanky body towering above his drug lord boss. He eyed Lucky, but she couldn't read his poker face. Briefly she wondered if he had helped Chavez kill her father.

Dominguez stood back against one wall and folded his arms across his chest. His mustache briefly twitched when he saw Lucky wriggling her fingers, trying to loosen the tape. He gave a slight shake of his head in warning. She glared at him.

"Looks like you aren't so lucky today." Orozco smiled, his bushy mustache curving upward.

He stood a few feet in front of her. Lucky gauged the distance between her boot and his crotch, which was somewhat hidden by the oversized suit. She'd need him to step a little bit closer.

His pupils were dilated. Small globs of perspiration dotted his upper lip. She could see the pulse throbbing in the vein on his neck. His hands hung by his side and his fingers twitched.

Lucky took all of this in. Did Orozco sample his own wares or was it something else?

"Who are you?" he said, and stepped closer. "What is your real name? You're not who you said you were."

"I told you. My name is Lucky," she said lightly. "I got your money back. How else am I supposed to prove my loyalty?"

Orozco shook his head. "It's too late for that."

But he looked confused for a split second. "You don't check out. That wanted poster? My contacts couldn't find any banks you'd hit."

"Your contacts?" Lucky sneered. "They must suck."

Her eyes narrowed.

"Enough of these stupid games," she said. "Let me go now. I held up my end of the deal. I've more than proven myself to you."

Orozco leaned forward. Lucky looked down. He was still too far away for her boot to reach him. His face was now turning beet red.

"Nobody tells me what to do," he hissed. "You don't know who you're messing with."

A vein in his jaw throbbed.

Lucky didn't answer.

"I will let you go when I please, and it's not going to be until you tell me who you work for and where the big guy is."

He drew back a few feet, definitely out of range of Lucky's boot now.

"I'm only going to ask you one more time," he said. "Where's the big guy and who do you both work for?"

Lucky stared at him for a long moment.

Then, very slowly and very deliberately, she turned her head and spat on the ground. Then she raised an eyebrow in challenge.

With a speed that surprised Lucky, Chavez stepped forward and struck the side of her face, again sending her head reeling.

"You will talk," he said.

She lifted her leg, aiming her boot toward his crotch, but Chavez had retreated as quickly as he'd swooped in. Orozco paused at the door.

"She has ten fingers and ten toes," he said. "Let's start there."

Then he turned to Lucky. "You have twenty chances to answer. I think that should be more than sufficient."

He walked out with Dominguez following.

After the door slammed behind them, Lucky looked at Chavez.

"Just you and me now, *chico*," she said. "Think you can handle me?"

Chavez slowly withdrew a long Mexican bowie knife from a holder at his belt.

He held it up to his mouth and licked the side of the gleaming blade.

Lucky made sure to keep her face stone.

He took a step forward, tapping the blade on his open palm as he walked.

"You're lucky that I follow orders from *jefe*, otherwise, you would have a lot more to deal with than me chopping off your fingers and toes."

"Oh yeah?" Lucky smirked. "Like what?"

He grabbed his crotch and made an obscene thrusting gesture.

Lucky laughed scornfully and rolled her eyes.

"There's nothing down there for me to worry about."

In an instant, he was in front of her, holding the blade of his knife against her throat.

He was breathing heavily, his face red with anger.

"Go ahead and kill me." Lucky bit out the words, her eyes glued on his.

"See what Orozco thinks about that. See what he thinks about a *cabron pendejo* who can't follow simple orders."

Chavez drew back.

"I told you. When you can't get the information out of me, your days are numbered. He will no longer count on you. He will no longer trust you. He will have Dominguez torture you just like you're torturing me. I work for him too, and yet look what he's having you do? I'm responsible for getting him four hundred thousand dollars and yet now I'm the one tied up. Who says you'll be treated any better than me?"

"He trusts me inexplicably," he said.

Lucky burst into laughter. Chavez narrowed his eyes.

"What?"

"I think the word you are reaching for is 'implicitly,'" Lucky said. "But actually the other word makes more sense. It's difficult to believe he trusts you."

Chavez wrinkled his forehead in confusion as his face grew even redder.

But after a few seconds, he regained his composure.

"Tell me who your boss is and you can save your fingers and make me look good at the same time," he said. "And maybe your death won't be as painful as I could make it."

"We both know I'll probably tell you what you want before you have to draw blood," Lucky said in a smooth lie and swift change of tactic. "But first I'd like to know how you guys found out I wasn't who I said I was. I mean, you're a pretty smart guy. Was it you?"

Chavez shot her a look to see if she was mocking him but she was leaning forward, eyes soft, in an eager-to-listen pose.

"How?" Lucky asked, wide-eyed. "I thought I was solid."

Meanwhile, Lucky was keeping an eye on the monitor with the security camera footage. In one frame, she saw Orozco and Dominguez slide into a limousine and head out a dirt path behind the compound.

"*El jefe*, he knows that I'm invaluable, and if you tell me everything, I will finally get my shot."

"Why should I tell you? You said I'm dead anyway."

Chavez grinned at her, his mouthful of gold teeth flashing.

"You tell me now, I only rape you once, maybe twice, before you die."

"That's your best offer?" Lucky asked. "But I don't understand what the big deal is. I mean that politician and stuff? It seemed like that had nothing to do with us. Why bring us into this deal at all?"

"*El jefe* cannot be connected to Crenshaw. Not publicly. Crenshaw is going to become president with our help and then we will be kings in America."

Lucky laughed. "Okay. Good luck with that."

Chavez paced the room, so caught up in their conversation he didn't seem to notice Lucky's furious efforts to get free as she rotated her wrist back and forth to loosen the tape binding her to the chair.

All she needed was for Chavez to come a little closer with that knife. She hadn't managed to loosen the tape holding her individual fingers, but she'd worked the strip holding down her right wrist. Once her wrist was free, she could slip the fingers out of the remaining tape. At least that's what she hoped.

But she needed him to come close enough for her to get the knife.

She needed a distraction.

Lucky saw something else on the security cameras. The screen showed a cloud of dust on the horizon as a vehicle made its way down the long driveway toward the compound.

This might just be the break she'd been waiting for.

The vehicle was now close enough to see.

Lucky tried to hide her smile.

One distraction coming right up.

36

Adrenaline pumped furiously through Shepherd as he gunned the engine of the Hate Truck, barreling down the road and then swerving quickly to ram the large gate at the foot of the driveway.

After ripping it right off its hinges, the truck plowed down the driveway with the gate impaled on its front end until Shepherd slammed on the brakes and the truck fishtailed. The back end now faced a second gate that separated the driveway from the compound itself.

Shepherd leaped out of the truck and hopped onto its bed. Within seconds, he'd leaned down and grabbed a rocket-propelled grenade launcher. The RPG he fired exploded into the gate, blasting a clean hole through it.

He then took aim at the small army of men who scurried out of the compound, firing at the Hate Truck. Using the machine gun mounted on the bed, Shepherd managed to take out about half of the gunmen heading his way. The other half scattered and took cover.

With the gunmen dispersed, Shepherd had a chance to do what he did best: clear the enemy ranks in a quick, vicious, close-quarters combat gun battle.

The closest gunman was reloading his weapon. Shepherd took him out as he passed. After seeing movement out of the corner of his eye, Shepherd whirled and shot right through the driver's side window of the truck. The rounds shattered the window and continued through the cab to shatter the passenger side window before lodging in the neck of the gunman on the other side. He crumpled to the ground as Shepherd continued toward the compound's front door, shooting to his right and left, his hands crossing his body as he fired.

When he emptied the guns, he dropped them as he walked and reached behind him to the shotgun strapped to his back. Swinging that forward, he cleared another three to four men who charged out from their cover to stop him as he grew closer to the house.

Then a gunman came out of nowhere and ran toward Shepherd, yelling like a banshee and firing kamikaze-style. Shepherd's assault rifle easily stopped the man, but not before a few well-aimed bullets hit their mark, sending Shepherd reeling.

He ducked behind a truck and looked down with a groan.

Most of the rounds had struck his body armor, but his left bicep was bleeding profusely. Taking a folded bandana out of his pants pocket, he tied a quick knot over the wound with his right hand and his teeth.

He was only a few feet from the door. He needed to get inside and find Lucky.

They'd already had her way too long.

37

When Shepherd sent the RPG through the front gate, it was exactly the distraction Lucky had been waiting for.

Chavez was still standing in front of her when the explosion erupted. He swung his head toward the large monitor, giving Lucky a chance to rip her right hand free of the chair while simultaneously sliding her fingers out of the tape. She'd flexed and worked her fingers enough to loosen the tape so she could just slide them out once her wrist was free.

Before Chavez could react, Lucky grabbed his wrist and quickly twisted the knife blade toward his abdomen so when he whirled back around, his own body weight sent the blade plunging into his gut.

Eyes wide with astonishment, he looked up at Lucky as he fell to the ground.

Lucky tipped to one side so she could topple her chair. She fell heavily onto the concrete floor, but the impact was softened by the chair landing on Chavez's outstretched leg. Scooting, Lucky managed to get the knife and sliced through her other bindings.

As she did, she kept one eye on the monitor and watched as Shepherd laid waste to the cartel men trying to stop him.

The second she was free, she knelt down beside Chavez's face.

"Remember what I told you earlier?" she asked.

He looked at her with a blank expression.

"My father's name? It was Benito Luis Rodriguez."

Then she picked up his bowie knife and slit his throat.

Leaping to her feet, she ran to the door and tried the handle, but it was locked. She was about to search Chavez's body for keys when she looked up at the monitor and saw Shepherd race into the house. Running back to the door, she bellowed, "In here!" and pounded on it with her fists.

"Stand back!" Shepherd shouted.

She pressed herself against a side wall.

"All clear!" she shouted. She could see Shepherd raise a shotgun outside the door, and then the screen turned fuzzy as he blasted the lock off and some shrapnel flew up and took out the camera.

Lucky stepped into the center of the room, clutching the bloody bowie knife in front of her.

Shepherd's eyes roamed over her, looking for injuries. Only then did his glance go to Chavez's body. Then he looked back up at Lucky.

"You good?" he asked.

"I'm fine," Lucky said. "What took you so long?"

As soon as she said the words, her eyes grew wide, and she raised her arm and threw the knife. It whizzed past Shepherd's head.

A gunman who had been standing in the doorway sank to his knees wordlessly, the knife in his chest.

"Nice shot."

Lucky nodded.

"That's two for me."

Shepherd gave one of his small, sexy smirks but didn't answer.

Lucky jutted her chin toward the monitor. One of the security cameras showed the Hate Truck on fire. "We're going to need some other wheels."

Shepherd was already crouched down, rooting around in Chavez's pockets. He held up a keychain with a vehicle key on it.

"Let's get the hell out of here," Lucky said.

38

Orozco sank back into the limousine's leather seat and took a long drag on his cigar. He exhaled toward Dominguez, who was sitting across from him, eyes hidden behind aviator sunglasses.

"We're so close, Dominguez." Orozco rattled the ice in the bottom of his glass of tequila. He wordlessly handed the nearly empty glass to Dominguez.

The head of security plopped two more ice cubes into the glass and then poured in more tequila. He didn't say a word, but his movements were rigid and tense, as if he were a long-suffering wife waiting on an abusive husband.

After handing Orozco the glass, he sat back and turned his head to look out the window at the desert passing by in beige and brown flashes.

Absentmindedly, he rested his forearm on the leather duffle bag sitting on the seat beside him. It contained four hundred thousand dollars in cash. The payment to Crenshaw. After downing his tequila, Orozco chortled and reached over to pat Dominguez on the thigh.

"This meeting is going to change our lives," he said, more effusive than ever after having three glasses of tequila in the span of thirty minutes.

Dominguez slowly turned his head away from the window and looked pointedly down at the hand on his thigh. Orozco quickly removed it and sat back, still grinning.

He rubbed his palms together.

"Finally, I will have a civilized dinner with people of my caliber," he said, almost as if to himself. "I'm very much looking forward to it. The only thing that could make it better is if Mrs. Orozco could be there."

Then a frown creased his features. "I think that once this deal is done, an unfortunate accident needs to happen to her dear little dog. It has been sick one too many times. This is the last important event she will miss because of that dog. If I'm going to embark on a respectable new life, I need her at my side."

Dominguez gave a slow nod. Then he sighed.

Killing dogs was going too far in his opinion. If he was asked to do it, he would have to lie to his boss. He would pretend the dog was dead but find it another home. He disagreed, just like he did when Orozco scolded his men for letting the dark-haired girl's dog run away at the bank instead of incinerating the canine in a hail of bullets. There was no need for that. An innocent dog who never hurt anybody didn't deserve to die violently.

"Dominguez!"

He snapped out of his daydreams and looked at his boss.

"I was saying that we need to dress up for this dinner. When we get to the safe house, I want you to shower adequately. I took the liberty of buying you a new shirt and pants that I think will be more acceptable for the dinner party at Crenshaw's ranch."

"Thanks, *jefe*."

Orozco beamed in pride and gave a small nod as if he were acknowledging applause from an audience at a formal function.

Dominguez shifted uncomfortably and then frowned when his phone rang.

"Bueno?" he said.

A flurry of shouting met his words.

Lucky was gone. Everybody was dead.

Across the limousine, Orozco's smile faded as he watched Dominguez. The normally stoic head of security was stunned, his mouth open in shock, and then he closed his lips and shook his head in disappointment.

"Where are they now?"

Then, without a word, he hung up.

Orozco leaped out of his seat and leaned over Dominguez, breathing tequila into the other man's face. His eyes were wild with anger.

"She escaped," Dominguez said without flinching.

When the news sank in, Orozco shouted, "Chavez is dead! He's a dead man! And so is everybody else who was there and didn't do their jobs!"

"The big guy took care of that for you."

Orozco's face was nearly purple with rage. He clenched his fists and spluttered but no words came out. He sank back into his seat, his eyes slits.

"He's with her?" Orozco spat out the words.

Dominguez nodded.

"Where are they?"

Swallowing first, Dominguez paused before relaying the news. "Headed this way."

"Damn it! They'll ruin everything."

"No."

It was a simple, confident statement.

"You're right," Orozco said, rallying. "Tomlinson and his men are already on their way. We end this now."

39

Standing and facing the west, Tomlinson cracked his snake-tattooed knuckles.

By this time tomorrow, it would all be over. He'd be done dealing with these damn Mexicans. At least for a while.

Crenshaw seemed to think working with them was the answer.

And he had to admit that four hundred large wasn't anything to sniffle at, especially money that had been cleaned across the border first. Untraceable. Cold. Hard. Cash.

That would buy a lot of hookers and blow for an Old Preacher Boy, he thought to himself, grinning. But nah, what he really wanted was to build himself a big ole ranch house with horses roaming the property like they did here.

He turned to look at the house behind him. It wasn't bad, actually. He'd taken the liberty of doing a little pre-meeting tour of the house, ostensibly to check its security and scan for any cameras or wires that would indicate the place was bugged.

Of course, his boy, Kong, was the expert at that sort of stuff, but nobody needed to know that. Tomlinson just wanted to see how the Big Fancy Cartel Leader lived at his home in America.

He had to admit the ranch house was pretty well-fortified, which would be a must for Tomlinson's new home. He never knew where the enemy could come from. Even these cartel losers could turn on him and try to take everything he had. He didn't trust any foreigners as far as he could throw them.

The ranch house had some good features, like a jacuzzi tub in the master bath. But despite its obvious luxuries, this particular house stank. Like a dirty Mexican. Maybe a rich one, but still a Mexican who should be keeping to his own damn side of the border.

As Tomlinson thought this, he heard a distant noise. The gated entrance to the main road was around a corner blocked by trees, so a few seconds passed before he saw the approaching limousine with the tinted windows kicking up a trail of dirt and dust behind it.

Tomlinson faced the vehicle until it stopped a few feet away and the driver got out to open the back door.

Dominguez stepped out first and hitched up his pants by the gun belt. He looked at Tomlinson but didn't say a word.

He stood to one side with his hand casually resting on the butt of his gun, eyes glued to Tomlinson as Orozco clambered awkwardly out of the limo.

Once Orozco gained his footing, he ran a hand through his hair.

"Preacher," he said.

Tomlinson hooked his thumb behind him. "Nice ranch you got here, *amigo*."

His face darkening, Orozco walked up to the silver-haired preacher.

"We got a problem," he said in a low voice, even though there was nobody within earshot.

"Oh yeah," Tomlinson said, biting his lip. "You don't have the money? Again?"

"I got the money," Orozco scoffed. "We just have some company. Be here any second. And my men, they are, uh, tied up right now."

"You got men here," Tomlinson said.

"Not going to be enough," Orozco said. "I need yours, too."

"Who's coming?" Tomlinson said, and tensed.

Dominguez cleared his throat behind them. Orozco turned and nodded for him to speak.

"The big guy and his sidekick," Dominguez said, then looked down, clearly uncomfortable with revealing the news.

"I thought you had them taken care of?"

Orozco didn't answer but his left eye began to twitch.

Then Tomlinson laughed. "You're right. Your men aren't enough!"

Then he grew somber and shook his head.

"This ain't a problem. At least not for my men. It's a pain in my ass. But it's not a problem."

He let out a long whistle and Kong stepped off the porch. He'd been standing in the shadows. He walked down and stood before Tomlinson.

"Remember that pro-wrestler wannabe and that little Mexican girl from the revival who tried to mess everything up? Looks like they're back and headed our way."

Kong nodded. He reached for the radio clipped to his belt and spoke into it.

Across the yard, the thirty-foot-high barn door swung open and a convoy of large pickup trucks rolled out. Each of the four trucks had at least two men in the back holding shotguns.

The trucks parked in a line across the driveway, their engines running, sending a low rumble through the air.

All eyes faced the driveway.

Then Tomlinson's phone dinged.

He looked at it for a second and then turned to Orozco.

"Let's get ready to rumble."

40

The large Mercedes with the blacked-out windows rocketed down the dirt road heading north with nothing for miles around except large cactuses and buzzards.

"As much as I hated Chavez, he didn't have bad taste in cars." Shepherd grinned at Lucky. "This is like an old-school hooptie car except it cost a hundred times more."

"We're almost there," Lucky said, peering out the windshield at the road in front of them. It could barely be called a road. It was more like a path that cut a car-sized swath through the brush and sand of the Sonoran Desert.

"You sure about this?"

Lucky nodded. "Yeah. I'll tell you when to turn."

Shepherd was about to answer when Lucky said loudly, "Brake!"

He slammed on his brakes and they skidded for several feet before she shouted, "Right turn! Now!"

Shepherd cranked the wheel hard. The Mercedes got a few feet of air before it landed hard on a dry riverbed. There was a crunch of metal and their seatbelts locked up, but the vehicle seemed fine.

"You might have given me a little warning." Shepherd glared at Lucky.

"It's not like I come here every day," she said. "I told you as soon as I saw it."

Shepherd gave her a look that she ignored.

"Where to, Captain Kirk?" he asked.

"Keep going north. This is going to take us across the border near Candelaria, Texas. From there we won't be far from the safe house."

Then she scowled and mumbled, "Captain Kirk."

"Better than Captain Hook," he quipped.

"True," she said. "Because that would make you Smee."

"Touché," he said.

Shepherd's phone dinged and he looked down.

"Red said Tomlinson's gang is also at the safe house."

Lucky stared at him for a second and then burst into tears.

Stunned, Shepherd pulled to a stop.

"Is there something you need to tell me?" he asked.

Angrily, she swiped at the tears streaking her face. "Thought the old cowboy was dead, that's all."

She turned away to face the windshield.

"Not yet," Shepherd said, and stepped on the gas.

"Good," she said in a soft voice.

"How much further until we can cross the border."

"There." She pointed to a spot where the thick brush lining the riverbed opened up. "That's Texas right there."

Slowing the Mercedes, Shepherd turned the wheel toward the slight hill leading out of the riverbed and through the opening. Once the car popped through, there was another slightly worn path through the desert brush.

Ten minutes later, they exited onto the highway.

"Boom," he said.

Lucky looked at the map on the car's dashboard monitor.

"How handy that Chavez had the directions to the safe house plugged in."

"Convenient," Shepherd said. "What's our ETA?"

"Ten minutes."

"Wish we had something more than these shotguns," he said.

They'd scooped up the guns from the house before they'd left.

"A shotgun can cause a hell of a hole in a man," Lucky said.

"True, but I've got a feeling we're going to need a whole lot of shotguns where we're going."

A few miles later, Shepherd slowed the vehicle to a crawl.

"It's right there," Lucky said, pointing to a gate further down the road.

"What's the move?" Shepherd asked.

"Storm the castle?"

Then the car's dashboard map showed they had arrived.

Lucky hit "End Route" as Shepherd pulled over to the side of the road across from the compound gate.

Shepherd looked out at the cattle and horses grazing on the large farm across the road. He frowned.

"That's odd," he said.

"What?" Lucky turned to look.

"Those two horses. They are tied to the fence with bridles and saddles."

"No real rancher would do that in a million years," Lucky said.

"That's what I was thinking," Shepherd said. "It's pretty damn convenient."

"There are no coincidences," Lucky said, and opened her car door.

"How good are you at horseback riding?"

"Fair to middlin'," she said in a deep Southern accent.

A few minutes later, Shepherd was leading the horses out to the road.

He put his interlaced palms together to give Lucky a lift onto the horse, but she winked and threw herself onto its bare back, easily straddling it.

He handed her the reins to the other horse.

She lifted an eyebrow.

"Remember that time in Istanbul?" he asked.

Lucky frowned and looked from the car to the ranch's front gate and back again.

"I could just pick the lock?" she offered.

"We need a distraction."

A few minutes later, Shepherd slammed the door of the Mercedes as it barreled toward the ranch's gate. He ran over, hopped onto the back of his horse, and yelled, "Let's go!"

They dug their heels into the sides of the horses and leaned forward as they picked up speed. After the horses reached a fast gallop, Shepherd steered his toward a four-foot fence. "I got another question," he called over his shoulder as he dug his heels into the side of the horse. "How good are you at jumping horses?"

"The question is how good are you?" she yelled.

After Shepherd's horse cleared the fence, she gave a loud whoop as her horse sailed over it behind him.

As they landed, the Mercedes crashed into the gate to their left. They kept their horses racing near a line of trees while several trucks from the ranch sped toward the crashed Mercedes.

Tattooed men balancing in the truck beds leaned out and fired at the Mercedes. Within seconds, the car had crashed into a tree. The trucks descended on it, peppering it with bullets until it was smoking and the engine had caught fire.

When the first two trucks full of gunmen reached the Mercedes, they realized it was empty.

But only when two of the men standing there slumped to the ground did they realize they were under attack.

Shepherd and Lucky charged on horseback, firing shotguns with one hand.

They split the first truck, riding up on opposite sides and firing until it crashed into a piece of farm equipment. But the other three trucks were quickly on them, tearing through the rutted fields.

Shepherd was turned around, firing at a gunman shooting at Lucky, so he didn't see another truck come to a screeching halt in front of him.

His horse halted, reared up, and threw him before it bolted.

Shepherd landed hard near the truck's passenger door. He quickly rolled up against the truck but was too bulky to roll underneath.

At first, the man in the passenger seat was confused. He looked outside his window for Shepherd's body but couldn't see anything. Then he saw Shepherd in his side window and grinned. Rolling down his window, he leaned out and turned, ready to shoot Shepherd. But Shepherd was already gone, crawling toward the back of the truck.

The man aimed his gun but then fell forward with a bullet to his forehead.

Lucky's second shot took out the driver.

She yanked on the reins a few feet before she reached the truck.

"Come on!" she yelled at Shepherd.

He sprinted forward, easily hopping onto the back of the horse behind Lucky and grabbing hold of her waist.

"You're welcome," she said over her shoulder in the wind. "That's three for me."

"My turn next," he said into her ear.

Lucky dug her heels into the side of the horse hard, pushing the sweating beast as the fourth truck approached. They were cut off on both sides, and a fence and a ditch lay before them. It looked like they were trapped.

"Maybe we should turn around and charge them," Shepherd said, leaning close to Lucky.

"Nah. We got this. Hold on tight!" she shouted, heading straight for a small fence.

They cleared it easily, and the truck behind them skidded to a stop.

Now they were at the back of the property. A large wall surrounding the backyard was lined with barbed wire, and a man with a machine gun was walking atop it. He suddenly swiveled and faced them.

"To your six," Lucky said over her shoulder.

Shepherd rested the butt of the rifle on her shoulder and fired. The guard toppled off the wall.

Then Lucky slowed the horse to a trot, followed by a stop.

They both hopped off. Lucky patted the horse on the head.

"Thank you, my friend."

Then Shepherd slapped its butt and it took off toward a line of trees at the back of the compound.

"I thought you said 'fair to middlin',' but you rode that horse like a champ," he said.

"You seem to forget I grew up on a farm," Lucky said. "You're looking at the 2002 Escaramuza Champion."

"The escargot what?"

"A female *charrería*."

"Layman's terms, Lucky."

"The goddamn queen of the rodeo."

"Yee-haw!"

41

Lucky was already at the back wall of the ranch.

They needed to get inside.

That's where Orozco would be hiding out.

"I'll go left, you go right," Shepherd said.

As they drew closer, a back door flew open and Dominguez emerged, guns blazing. Lucky took cover around the side of the wall but Shepherd was still in the open.

Dominguez set his sights on Shepherd and marched steadily toward him, firing as he went. Shepherd darted toward a rickety shed for cover. Once his body was shielded, he peered out and fired, nearly hitting Dominguez.

The cartel man ducked and raced back inside the door to the walled backyard.

Shepherd took advantage of Dominguez's retreat to run forward and position himself behind a green tractor.

Lucky crept back around the wall. At the same time, a few of Tomlinson's men rounded the opposite corner and fired wildly.

Lucky picked off a few of them, and the rest momentarily retreated while she laid down a line of protective fire.

That gave Shepherd a chance to dart through the door to the walled backyard and take shelter behind a huge outdoor stone fireplace.

Shepherd moved with his back against the wall, scanning for any sign of Dominguez.

He'd just reached the ranch house's back door when he saw Dominguez rise up from behind a small bar area attached to a swimming pool. Shepherd had a clear shot. He lifted his gun, his finger about to squeeze the trigger, when he was yanked by the collar from behind and flung through the back door of the compound. His gun clattered to the tile floor as he tried to regain his balance and was met with a meaty fist to the jaw.

Seconds before the blow found its mark, Shepherd saw who his attacker was.

Kong.

Recovering quickly from the punch, Shepherd launched himself at Kong, head-butting the other man and sending them both flying into an end table that shattered into fragments under them.

Shepherd recovered first and had just managed to get back on his feet when Kong swung a poker from the fireplace in a sweeping motion. He jumped back, the poker merely grazing his legs instead of crushing his kneecaps.

Shepherd lunged forward and stepped on the poker, bringing it down to the ground.

Kong was up and charging Shepherd now, his fists flying right and left. A few of the punches landed on Shepherd's head as he barreled toward the other man, head down, going for the solar plexus.

Shepherd was now a fist-whirling machine, pummeling the other man relentlessly while Kong could do nothing except try to push Shepherd's head away from where it was buried in his chest.

Shepherd bashed his knee into the other man's groin, and Kong fell heavily, curling up in the fetal position.

Within seconds, Shepherd had whirled and was on the ground behind Kong, an elbow looped around the other man's neck. His face growing red as he struggled for breath, Kong managed to stretch out an arm and lift a gun off the floor. He aimed it behind him and was just about to fire it into

Shepherd's face when Shepherd executed a swift move that instantly snapped Kong's neck.

He slumped to the ground.

Breathing heavily, Shepherd stood and flew out the back door.

Lucky was standing in the backyard, also breathing heavily, dirt streaked across her face and hair messy in a half-cocked ponytail.

"Dominguez?" Shepherd asked.

"I couldn't find him," she said. "I was busy with some of Tomlinson's men, and when I turned around he was gone."

"Looks like they're back," Shepherd said.

Four men sprinted around the corner, firing.

Lucky and Shepherd turned toward the back door, but two gunmen were coming from that direction.

Left with no other choice, they darted toward a crumbling outbuilding.

They made it behind the structure seconds before another half dozen men arrived in the back. Lucky peeked out from behind the shed to take a shot, but when she fired, nothing happened. Her gun was empty. She gave Shepherd a look of dismay.

He glanced down at his own weapon and shook his head.

"We're in trouble, Lady Luck."

"It's not looking great."

"Remember Kuwait?"

"Yeah. I saved your ass that time."

"Ha," he said. "More like I saved yours."

Lucky didn't argue.

The heavy onslaught of gunfire was starting to take off pieces of the structure around them. They huddled in the middle where a steel plate made up a back wall.

"They're going to realize any second now that we're out of ammo," Lucky said in a small voice. Shepherd nodded, his face somber.

They exchanged a long look, filled with things never said and chances never taken.

The moment was broken by a familiar voice.

"You're done for," Orozco yelled. "Drop your weapons and surrender and I'll spare your life. Whoever you're protecting isn't worth it. I know this isn't just you two acting alone. Tell me everything and I'll protect you from them. I have very, very powerful people on my side now."

"That's not the way I'm going out," Shepherd said.

"Me neither." Lucky shook her head.

The sun was setting to the west and the sky had turned neon red streaked with pink.

The light cast their faces in a golden glow.

"It's so beautiful," Lucky said.

"I know," Shepherd responded, his eyes on her.

She quickly looked away. "What now?"

He shook his head.

"Seems sort of a dumb way to die. Sort of anticlimactic."

She gave a strangled laugh. "It would've been much more exciting to die when we were in Bosnia. At least then it would have made sense and no one would've blamed us for not making it out."

"True," Shepherd said. "Plus the beaches in Bosnia are the bomb. I remember a particularly great night on a Bosnian beach."

They locked eyes. He reached for her cheek and his fingers had just grazed her skin when her eyes widened.

"What's that?" she said.

It was a low, familiar rumble.

Suddenly, the attack on them halted. The air grew silent except for the distant purr of what sounded like dozens of motorcycles. The ground began to shake.

"You've got to be kidding!" Lucky said. "How did they even know we were here?"

Shepherd shrugged. "I must've made quite an impression on the leader of the 12 Locas."

Lucky scoffed. "Max must have sent them."

"Or," Shepherd said with a smile, "Petra Torres wanted to see me again."

"I doubt that." Lucky rolled her eyes.

"You jealous?" he asked.

"Hell no," Lucky said. "Let's get this party started."

42

As the sound of the approaching biker gang grew closer, Tomlinson's men turned and ran toward the front of the house.

Lucky and Shepherd followed, darting from one structure to the other to stay covered.

As they rounded the house, they had a clear view of dozens of motorcycles jumping over the toppled front gate in a long, ominous line that was heading straight toward them.

A familiar green pickup truck brought up the rear of the pack.

"Is that?" Lucky said.

"Damn straight. It's Red!" Shepherd said with a whoop.

The older man came to a skidding stop that sent the truck fishtailing toward the house. Lucky raced over and hopped in the back. Red threw her a gun through the back window, and they both used the cab as cover as they fired at the onslaught of attackers, trying to provide cover for the bikers who were firing wildly and taking out Tomlinson's men.

Shepherd, who had stopped to pluck a shotgun off a dead cartel man, was on his way to the truck to join them when a man with a large machete knife stepped in front of him. By defending himself with the barrel of the empty shotgun, Shepherd was able to ward off the man's attempt to gut him, but he was clearly growing tired.

Shepherd was holding off the machete-yielding attacker with the shotgun barrel, each man breathing in the other's face, when Lucky spotted Dominguez leaning out an upstairs window above Shepherd.

He had a pistol aimed at Shepherd.

"Red!" Lucky shouted.

The older man immediately lifted his sniper rifle and fired.

Dominguez's body tumbled out the window and landed on top of the man with the machete, knocking him to the ground.

Shepherd looked down in surprise.

A second later, Orozco raced out of the house. He ran in the opposite direction, away from Shepherd.

As soon as she spotted him, Lucky jumped out of the truck bed and gave chase. Shepherd was a few steps ahead of her when a pickup truck flew around the corner.

The truck fishtailed to a stop by Orozco. Tomlinson was behind the wheel. Orozco pulled himself into the truck bed, and then Tomlinson gunned the engine and raced toward the main road.

Without a word, Lucky and Shepherd ran to a nearby truck and plucked the dead driver out onto the ground. Lucky climbed behind the wheel and they zoomed after Orozco and Tomlinson.

Now several bikers and an assortment of other vehicles were charging toward the main road. Tomlinson's truck looked ready to escape when a shot rang out. The truck jerked hard to the left, struck another vehicle, and then flipped and rolled wildly into the gate, hitting the Mercedes still stuck to it.

When they grew close, Lucky stopped the truck, and she and Shepherd hopped out, running toward the gate with their guns drawn. As they grew closer, they slowed and cautiously approached the overturned vehicle.

When they were about fifty meters away, Tomlinson emerged from the other side of the overturned vehicle, dragging Orozco by one arm. His other hand held a gun. He fired it at Lucky and Shepherd as he ran toward a live oak tree. He managed to reach it before Lucky and Shepherd could get close enough to take him out.

A few seconds later, Tomlinson broke cover and darted away from

Lucky and Shepherd, leaving Orozco behind the tree. From their position, they could see the drug lord's legs sticking out. He was not moving.

That's when Lucky realized Tomlinson was running for an overturned truck not far away. Several of his men were huddled behind it.

"He's going to get away!" she shouted.

As Tomlinson passed a large tree, a bullet struck the trunk centimeters away from his head. But no gunmen seemed to be within range.

Shepherd shaded his eyes to look for the sniper who almost hit Tomlinson.

Then he spotted him and nudged Lucky.

Silhouetted by the setting sun, a man in a cowboy hat stood against another tree, holding a rifle.

It was Red.

Even from a distance, Shepherd and Lucky could tell he was still badly injured and was using the tree to prop himself up. As they watched, he slumped to the ground.

Lucky made a small sound.

Shepherd took a step, but Lucky put her hand on his arm.

"Go after Tomlinson," she said. "I'll get Red."

As they split off, Lucky saw Orozco begin to limp back toward his limo.

As Shepherd sprinted toward Tomlinson, the remaining 12 Locas zipped around the ranch, picking off the last members of Tomlinson's Aryan army. The bikers were shouting and whooping with glee as they shot out the ranch house windows. A few passing bikers fired at the vehicle where Tomlinson was taking cover with some of his men. Right before Shepherd reached it, a bullet hit the gas tank and the vehicle burst into flames. The men taking cover behind it scattered.

Tomlinson took off, heading toward the limo that Orozco was driving.

Too late, he saw Shepherd coming full speed toward him.

They both raised their weapons at the same time.

"Vengeance is mine!" Tomlinson shouted. "For the day of their calamity is at hand!"

As the last word left his mouth, both men fired. Shepherd's bullet reached its target first and Tomlinson toppled to the ground, dead before his head hit the dirt.

43

"Red!" Lucky said as soon as she reached his side. "You're hurt."

"Just a flesh wound."

"How many times have you been shot?" she asked.

"Who's counting?" He winked.

"You don't look so good."

"Gee, thanks," he said wryly. Then he lifted his gun to point behind her. "Get out there. He's getting away."

Lucky turned to see Orozco fling his driver's body out of the limo and crawl into the driver's seat.

She hesitated, and Red said in a softer voice, "I got the bleeding to stop. I'll be fine for now. Go on."

He quickly reloaded his shotgun and handed it to her.

"Go on now. Get."

Reluctantly, she left Red and turned and ran. Orozco was gunning the limo toward the west. Lucky looked around.

The horse she'd been riding was nearby, racing around frantically, terrified by the gunfire. She gave a sharp whistle and it drew to a stop.

"It's okay, baby," she said as she grew closer. The animal's eyes were wild with fear.

Sweat had frothed on its limbs.

"Come on, girl," Lucky said, coaxing it toward her.

Then Lucky was beside it, stroking its nose while keeping her eye on the limo. Orozco had slowed down to navigate through a rocky patch of boulders in the field beside the ranch house.

Just then a woman on a motorcycle stopped in front of her.

It was Petra Torres.

Lucky eyed her warily but kept her shotgun at her side.

"You here to shoot me?" Lucky said.

"Nah." Petra smiled. "Wanted to know if you needed to borrow my bike?"

"You're kidding, right?" Lucky tilted her head.

"We badass bitches need to stick together."

Lucky's eyes widened.

"That's, um, awfully sweet, but I think I'm a better horse rider than biker. Thanks, though."

"No problem."

And then Petra Torres was gone.

Within seconds, Lucky was on the back of the horse, spurring it on with her heels dug into its sides, her right hand gripping the reins, her wounded left arm cradling the shotgun.

Urging the animal on with her thighs and whispering encouraging words in its ear, Lucky quickly caught up to the limo, which had nearly made it to a fence that bordered the main road.

Riding up behind the limo, Lucky managed to guide the horse straight with her thighs so she could use both hands to aim and fire Red's shotgun. But right when she squeezed the trigger, the horse nearly stumbled on a rut and she missed the limo entirely.

Grabbing hold of the reins again, she managed to catch up, and was galloping alongside the driver's side window when Orozco stuck a gun out and fired. But his aim also went wild as the limo bumped and bounced across the rocky, uneven terrain.

"You hurt this horse and I'll make sure your wife's death is slow and painful!" Lucky shouted.

He lifted his weapon and fired at her point blank, his eyes full of hatred.

But the chamber was empty. He tossed the gun out the window and jerked the wheel so the limo swerved toward Lucky.

As Lucky gave a violent yank on the reins to avoid the car hitting them, the horse balked and began to rear up. She quickly leaned down and spoke into its ear, calming it as they continued to give chase alongside the limo.

Ahead of them was the fence. Lucky spurred the horse faster and urged it to jump. It easily leaped over the fence seconds before the limo tore through it, taking huge swaths of its metal links down with it. Then they were across the main road and on another property.

Too late, Lucky spotted a steep ravine in front of them. There was no way that the horse could jump it and no way the limousine could traverse it. She looked over. Orozco had found another gun and was pointing it right at her, waiting for his shot, his eyes flicking back and forth between her and the ravine. The bumpy terrain bounced the limo up and down but he still managed to squeeze off a shot. It missed her but skimmed the back of the horse's neck.

Lucky glared at him.

"I told you to keep the horse out of it," she shouted.

Then, keeping her eyes locked on Orozco, she lifted the shotgun hidden in her other hand. His eyes widened. But it was too late.

She squeezed the trigger. Orozco slumped in his seat, and the limousine veered wildly and struck a large boulder right before the ravine.

Orozco's body was catapulted through the windshield and into the ravine. The limousine followed suit and flipped, flying into the ravine on top of Orozco and then exploding loudly before bursting into flames.

44

The biker gang had ridden off into the sunset.

Petra Torres had loaded the bodies and bikes of the fallen into the back of a pickup truck.

Lucky stood back when Shepherd went over to help.

She watched as Shepherd bowed his massive body down to the petite gang leader as they spoke. A few minutes later, the two fist-bumped.

Torres hopped on her bike and gave a long, piercing whistle with an arm movement above her head. Then the pickup and bikes started up and headed toward the road.

Within sixty seconds, they were a distant memory.

Shepherd walked back to stand by Lucky and Red, who were sitting on the tailgate of Red's truck.

Smoking vehicles and bodies were scattered around the ranch. The house behind them had all its windows shot out and the front door torn off its hinges.

Surveying the carnage, Lucky shook her head.

"Well that could've gone better."

"Could've gone a lot worse," Red responded.

"True that, old-timer," Shepherd said.

"Hey, who you calling old?"

Red's words were drowned out by the bone-chattering whomp of rotor blades. The three looked up. To the west, against a sky turning purple, a fleet of large military helicopters were headed their way. Within moments, the helicopters had landed and men in tactical gear jumped out, screaming and pointing assault rifles at them.

"Holy mother of?" Red thrust his arms in the air, fingers spread.

"Little late," Lucky said in a low voice.

"It's called covering their ass," Red quipped.

Shepherd and Lucky exchanged a glance and stuck their hands up in the air, too, as the men approached.

Tensing, Shepherd said to Lucky, "You know I can't get arrested."

"I think we're good."

"You think? You think? That's not good enough," Shepherd said.

"Hands up!" an armed soldier shouted in Lucky's face.

"I can't get them up any more than they are," she said.

"You think this is funny, girl?"

"The only thing that's going to be funny is when your superior officer fires your ass for calling me 'girl,' soldier."

He sneered but didn't respond.

Another soldier cuffed the three of them and walked them toward the ranch's front porch. They were guarded by four armed soldiers as the rest of the men from the helicopter rounded up the few members of Tomlinson's and Orozco's crews who were still alive. They made them crouch against a truck near the driveway.

Ten minutes later, another helicopter approached.

This one was all black with a nose that looked like the head of a catfish. It barely made any sound as it swooped in and landed.

"What in the?" Shepherd squinted into the sky. "Black Hawk?"

"Nah." Red shook his head, smiling. "It's a RAH-66 Comanche."

"No kidding?" Shepherd said.

Red let out a low whistle. "Sells for a cool fifteen million. Fires 20 mm cannon rounds and air-to-air or air-to-ground missiles."

"I thought the military terminated the Comanche program—too expensive," Shepherd said.

"Nothing's too expensive for our friend," Lucky said.

A man with a crewcut and black fatigues jumped out of the helicopter and headed directly toward the front porch.

"Uncuff them," he said as soon as he reached the foot of the steps.

"Sir?" The soldier who had called Lucky "girl" scrunched up his face.

Another soldier stepped forward. He was holding a cell phone and his voice was shaking as he said, "Do as he says. I just got a call from the colonel. They are to be released at once."

"Yes, sir," the other man said.

After their handcuffs were removed, Lucky pointed at Red.

"He needs medical attention stat."

The man with the crewcut nodded and yelled, "Medic."

As soon as he spoke, a soldier raced over from one of the helicopters with a first aid kit.

"I told you I'm fine," Red grumbled, but he didn't protest when the medic told him to sit on the porch for a second.

"Get him loaded up and to the nearest hospital," the man with the crewcut said, nodding at Red.

"I'm good," Red said, trying to stand and then nearly falling over.

Shepherd caught him. "Come on, my friend," he said. "Let's get you onboard one of these birds and get you all fixed up."

Red rolled his eyes but let Shepherd and the soldier help him to the helicopter.

Lucky leaned over and kissed Red's cheek. "See you soon."

As soon as the helicopter lifted off, the man with the crewcut turned to Lucky and Shepherd.

"This way," he said.

They followed him to the Comanche.

"Hop in. I've got orders to make a special delivery—one Shepherd and one Fox."

"Fox?" Shepherd raised an eyebrow as he looked at Lucky. "I mean I guess it's better than the Big Bad Wolf."

She shrugged. "I don't make up the code names."

"With an operation named Henhouse, we needed a fox," the man said.

They climbed into the Comanche and strapped in.

The man with the crewcut handed them black hoods.

"No offense, but the pilot is taking you to a secret location. It's protocol. Uncle Max asked that you keep the hood on until you land."

Shepherd frowned but pulled the hood on.

Lucky waited a beat and then pulled hers on as the helicopter took off.

"This better be good," she mumbled.

45

Lucky ripped off her hood as soon as the helicopter touched down.

She hopped out of the helicopter and looked around in surprise. They had landed on a helipad on the backend of the biggest yacht she'd ever seen. She swiveled her head. There was nothing around them for as far as the eye could see except turquoise seas.

"What the?" Shepherd said from beside her.

Three men in white uniforms stood with their arms behind their backs.

"Welcome," one man with a French accent said.

Another man walked up to them and handed them warm, damp towels.

"For your face?" he said.

Lucky took the towel and looked down at her hands, which were black with blood. She could just imagine how her face looked. She glanced at Shepherd. Yep. If she looked as bad as him, it would explain the stewards' expressions—a combination of fear and revulsion.

"Please follow me and we will show you to your rooms," the man with the French accent said. "We have a snack and water in there for you. Please feel free to bathe, nap, and then when you are ready, dress for dinner and meet in the saloon."

"Okay," Lucky said, and glanced at Shepherd. He made a face and shrugged.

After a long shower and quick nap, Lucky poked her head out her cabin door and looked at Shepherd's cabin across the hall. Quickly, she crossed and knocked on the door.

No answer.

She knocked again. Nothing. So she pounded it hard and hissed, "Shepherd!"

The door flung open and Shepherd stood there.

He was only wearing a towel wrapped around his waist, and his face had shaving cream on one cheek. He was holding a razor.

Lucky had slipped on a simple green velvet gown and pulled her hair back in a loose ponytail. Dressing up this much for dinner felt ridiculous, but she didn't have a choice. It was the only clothing item in her room. The clothes she'd arrived in were shredded and covered with blood and guts.

A silk suit hung on a hanger behind Shepherd.

"You going to wear that?" she asked, and pointed.

"Unless I wear this towel, I don't really have a choice."

"Same."

"I'm almost ready. Give me five."

He stepped into the hall a few minutes later.

"Where's the saloon?" she said in a loud whisper.

"No clue," he said.

At the end of the hall was a door and a short flight of steps. At the top of the steps stood the steward with the French accent.

"I hope you are well rested. I will show you to the saloon."

"Thank God," Lucky whispered.

Another small flight of stairs led them to the saloon, a massive open room with a dining table that could seat twenty and a small sitting area.

"Please have a seat," the steward said, and walked out.

They shot each other looks.

Shepherd remained standing but Lucky sank into a pink velvet chair.

The minutes passed. A black marble end table held a stack of magazines. The one on top had a picture of a tall, thin, handsome Indian man with smiling eyes and shoulder-length wavy hair. The caption said, "Wealthiest man in the world."

Lucky picked up the magazine and thumbed through it.

"Don't tell me you're actually reading that?" Shepherd said.

She smirked.

"You must be really bored to waste your time reading about a bunch of rich guys," he said.

"Maybe if the company wasn't so boring..."

"Haha," Shepherd said.

Lucky ignored him, and kept reading.

"But seriously," Shepherd said, "how can you read that? Are you reading about the guy on the cover, what's his face, the richest man in the world? That your type?"

Lucky flipped the magazine over and examined the man on the cover.

"I don't really think about how much money a guy has," she said.

"You're not answering the question. Is he your type?"

Lucky shrugged. "I don't have a type. But I like his smile. And I really like his hair."

"He needs a haircut," Shepherd said.

"You're just jealous he has hair."

A throat cleared and they both turned.

A tall, slim, handsome Indian man with shoulder-length wavy hair stood in the doorway. He was barefoot. He wore shorts and an unbuttoned white shirt, and a strange tattoo that looked like a keyboard covered his left forearm.

"You like my hair?" he said. "Thanks. I got hooked on watching hockey this past winter and wanted to see what I looked like if I had some 'flow' going on."

Their eyes widened.

The man stepped forward and stuck out his hand. "It's nice to finally meet you in person. I'm Jay Ravi. I think you know me better as Uncle Max."

46

"Please join me for an aperitif before dinner." He gestured toward the huge marble table in the center of the room. The dining room was surrounded by windows on three sides. To the west, a picture-perfect sunset bathed the entire room in a soft pink and orange glow.

After a steward poured them each a glass of champagne, Uncle Max held up his glass in a toast.

"I hope by now you can understand why I decided to bring you two back together again in your work for The Foundation," he said. "I know things went south for a while, but you can't argue that your teamwork in places like Angola and Belarus and Kuwait was top notch."

Neither Shepherd nor Lucky would look at each other.

"I know a lot's changed since then," he continued, "but I always thought you were better as a team than alone."

"Where's Red?" Shepherd asked.

"He's doing great. Stand by."

Uncle Max held out his left forearm and touched the tattoo. His forearm lit up in LED lights, and he pressed a few different illuminated buttons on his skin.

A large screen came down on one wall. He looked up at Lucky and Shepherd.

"Do you like my digital tattoo?" he asked. "It's a silicon and silk implant. It unlocks my car and house, monitors my blood sugar level, and can even act like an AirDrop that allows me to transfer information to your phone or other technology."

Suddenly, Red's face filled the large white screen.

"Hey! What's up, you two?" he said. "I see you finally met Uncle Max."

Shepherd shot Lucky a look. She shrugged.

"You look like you're doing well," Uncle Max said.

Red turned the phone away and a young woman with blonde hair nodded. "He's doing remarkably well," she said.

"Check out this place," Red said.

Red angled the screen so they could see he was in a hospital room with windows overlooking a turquoise bay. Three medical personnel were standing at a bank of monitors. A big TV screen that filled one wall was playing *Die Hard*. A long table was filled with a buffet of food and drinks.

"What kind of hospital is that?" Lucky asked.

"I spare no expense for my best team," Uncle Max said.

"Doc says I can go home in the next day or two," Red said. "But I might milk it an extra day. This place is growing on me."

"That's right," the woman said. "Now if you don't mind, I was just about to run some tests. Can Red call you later?"

"Of course." Uncle Max touched a button on his arm. The screen went black.

A steward in a white tuxedo paused near Shepherd and held out a silver tray with bacon-wrapped figs.

Shepherd took one and stuffed it in his mouth.

"Not bad," he said.

"What made you do this?" Lucky asked, and scrunched up her face. "All these ops you send us on? Why form The Foundation? Why do you care?"

Uncle Max threw back his head and laughed. "That's what I've always liked about you, Lucky. You aren't afraid to be direct."

Shepherd smirked. "That's an understatement," he said, and took a quick drink of his champagne as Lucky shot him a dirty look.

"I was the youngest billionaire in the world," Uncle Max said. "I was king of the world. I had everything you could ever dream of. The most alluring, beautiful women I had ever seen wanted to marry me. I had invitations from presidents, princes, prime ministers. My friends were heads of the most influential companies on the planet. I had it all."

He paused, then turned his head and looked right into the setting sun for a few seconds. Then he turned back to the table.

"And then the unthinkable happened. My sister's daughter, the most angelic little girl on earth, was diagnosed with cancer. Lung cancer. She was eight."

Lucky shook her head.

"At first, I went into fight mode. I was up for twenty-four hours researching top specialists. I was convinced that we could win this war. I had my private jets and helicopters on standby and flew Manisha around the world to receive care. I fought until the last second. When she died, I was in her hospital room with my sister and brother-in-law. It wasn't until the nurse said she had passed that I finally accepted that being the world's youngest billionaire didn't mean anything when it came to saving Manisha's life."

"I'm so sorry," Lucky said.

Shepherd shook his head and swiped at his eyes.

"I sank into a deep depression. I never left my house. I stayed holed up in my office playing video games. In that manufactured reality, I could be the hero. I could save little girls. I could save the world! I spent eight months in the dark.

"Then, one day, my sister came to see me. She handed me a newspaper article. It showed that three other children who lived in the same area as my niece had also been diagnosed with lung cancer. It was a cluster. The investigative journalist who wrote the article had linked the cluster with studies showing the ground water was contaminated with arsenic. This reporter linked the arsenic with a pharmaceutical company upriver from the town—Cyminix Labs."

"Crenshaw's company," Shepherd said.

Uncle Max closed his eyes for a second and nodded.

"Dr. Feel Good," he said. "When I first looked into him, I found that he was working on a deal with the cartel. The man tapped to be the next president was working to open the flow of drugs into America. So at first we went after him legally. But he was too powerful. Someone was protecting him. Someone even more powerful than me. I had to find another way to bring him down. I even tried having a private meeting with him and he laughed in my face."

"Looks like you had the last laugh," Shepherd said.

"So it would seem." Uncle Max plucked a cube of steak off a tray from one of the stewards. After he chewed it and swallowed, he winced. "That pharmaceutical plant was shut down earlier today by the EPA. And Crenshaw is going to be locked up for a long time. So one point for me, but my crusade isn't over yet.

"You see, when I dug deep into Crenshaw's world, I found out that I had been unwittingly contributing to his campaign coffers for years. For years! I had funded the monster who killed Manisha, the heartless megalomaniac who was killing children and laughing about it."

"But you didn't know," Lucky said. "You had no way of knowing."

"I should have known where my money was going," Uncle Max said. "Because the deeper I dug, the more I discovered that indirectly, I had been funding the worst sort of people and organizations on this earth—my money had been used to fund private wars, to destabilize entire countries. I have so much blood on my hands."

He closed his eyes again, then exhaled deeply before continuing.

"These revelations have changed my life. Now I know why I was put on this earth—to right the wrongs of the world using people like you to help me. I formed The Foundation to go after monsters who are too powerful to be stopped in any other way. People who are untouchable by local, federal, international governments. It's up to me to stop them. With your help, of course," he said, and held up a glass of champagne in a toast.

"We'll help all right," Lucky said. "You can count on us."

"I know." He gave a wan smile. "I'm going to be keeping you busy. You see, the more I dug into my accounts, the more I realized that I have a lot of reconciling to do. But I'm a patient man. One thing at a time. I will take them all down one by one."

He paused and looked out the window as the sound of an approaching helicopter filled the air.

He stood and reached for his jacket.

"I'll leave you two now. The captain will take you wherever you please. I have opened up Swiss bank accounts for each of you. From now on, money will never be an issue for you. I take very good care of my teams. Especially ones that have been brought into the inner circle like you two. But for now, try to enjoy yourselves. Rest up. You're going to need it because I'm going to keep you busy. Very, very busy."

EPILOGUE

A cantina outside Juarez

The mariachi band that had been playing raucously in the corner took a break, and the cantina filled with the sounds of people laughing and talking. The walls were hung with framed, faded yellow posters of bullfighting matches and famous Mexican singers. Red and green paper flags were strung against the low ceiling. The surface of the bar was covered with *loteria* cards that had been shellacked onto the ancient wood.

Red and Shepherd were reminiscing about the day they met in that bar.

"So glad my death wish didn't come true that day," Red said, and took a slug of his beer. "I had no idea what crazy-ass adventures you had in store for me."

The two men stopped talking and watched Lucky as she walked over to the bar.

The only sign of the violence from a few weeks earlier was the bandage on her arm and a scab on her cheek.

Red walked with a limp now—that he claimed was temporary—and Shepherd had a faded bruise on his jaw and a small scab on his forehead.

"That one cleans up nice," Red said in a matter-of-fact voice, nodding at

Lucky, who was laughing and joking with the older woman manning the bar.

Shepherd shrugged. "Heh."

"What's that?" Red smiled. "You don't agree?"

"I don't know."

Red chortled. Then he began laughing so hard that he threw back his head and clutched his stomach.

Frowning, Shepherd looked down into his beer and shook his head.

A smile spread across Lucky's face as she returned to the table. "What's so funny?"

Red finally gained control of his laughter, swiping at a few stray tears.

He reached out and clapped Shepherd on the back.

"Our friend here. Sometimes he just won't own up to what the rest of the world knows is true."

"Tell me about it," Lucky said.

"Enough," Shepherd said. "I know you two get off on ganging up on me, but give a guy a break."

"What won't you own up to?" Lucky asked in a teasing voice.

Shepherd shifted uncomfortably. "Nothing."

Red laughed. "Tell her."

Shooting daggers at Red, Shepherd shook his head and took a gulp of his beer.

"No, really? Wait, are you blushing?" Lucky quickly looked from Red to Shepherd. "Tell me what's going on."

"It's nothing," Shepherd said, and then looked at Lucky. "Hey, did I hear right? Did you actually break into Orozco's house? Fast Eddie said there was a break-in during the funeral. Cameras caught a burglar wearing a stocking cap. They said it was a woman."

"Pshaw," Lucky said. "What else did Fast Eddie have to say?"

"He said it was kind of strange because nothing was taken."

"Nothing?" Lucky said archly, and brushed her long hair back from her clavicle.

Shepherd looked down at her neck.

"Aha," he said, and smiled. "Glad to see you got your necklace back."

Lucky nodded and took a long sip of her beer. "There was never a question of me *not* getting it back."

"I believe that," Red said.

"Look." Lucky gave a slight nod toward the TV hanging above the bar.

"'Bout time," Red said.

The footage was from a news station reporting how US presidential hopeful Bill Crenshaw had been arrested and charged with ten felony counts, including conspiracy to launder narcotics proceeds, accessory to murder, bank fraud, conspiracy to violate administration regulations, and six other charges.

A polished news anchor with shellacked black hair and Superman cheekbones was on the screen.

"Authorities are tight-lipped about exactly which government organization was behind a deep cover mission that involved hired mercenaries working with the Mexican police," he said. "The undercover sting operation, dubbed Operation Henhouse, linked future presidential hopeful Bill Crenshaw with the Orozco Cartel. The name of the organization behind the covert operation is redacted in the official indictment—something we've never seen before. The indictment claims that the politician spent the drug money freely, believing it was laundered.

"Further investigation revealed that when Crenshaw was taken into custody, authorities found marked bills in the politician's own wallet with serial numbers directly linked to dead cartel leader Victor Orozco. Authorities seized Crenshaw's assets, believed to be worth two billion dollars. There's over one hundred million dollars alone linked to banks owned by both Orozco and Crenshaw. They'd planned to use it to buy their way into the White House."

Red let out a long whistle. "That would buy someone a lot of *cerveza*," he said, and held up his beer bottle.

They all laughed. Then Red grew serious and cleared his throat.

"I actually arranged this meeting on behalf of Uncle Max."

"And here I thought you missed me," Shepherd said.

Red made a face.

"Uncle Max thinks you two are better as a team than working alone," he said, and paused.

"He mentioned that already," Lucky said, and took a swig of her beer.

"You know, Lucky, the world's a safer place when you have a couple people you can trust at your side."

Sighing loudly, Lucky nodded. "Guess it's been a long time since I had people I could trust around me."

Red looked at Shepherd. "Maybe it's time for you both to stop flying solo. This lone wolf shit is getting old."

Shepherd pressed his lips together, but a smile crossed his face.

"So?" Red asked.

"Yeah, so?" Lucky raised an eyebrow.

Shepherd looked from one face to the other and nodded.

"Only if you're around to cover our six," he said to Red.

"Well, at least we already have our code names," Lucky said.

Red smiled. "Good." He patted the table. "Glad that's settled. Because there's plenty of people willing to pay good money for the kind of help you two can provide."

The three of them sat silently for a few seconds, drinking their beers.

After they finished, Shepherd stood. "My turn to buy."

"Nah." Red pushed back from the table. "You two are even, it's my turn." They both watched him walk away.

"Are we?" Shepherd asked, looking at Lucky.

"Are we what?" She made a face.

"Even?" he said. "Way I figure it, I saved your ass three times and you saved mine the same number."

A slow smile spread across her face.

"Yeah. Okay. I'll buy it. We're even." Then she paused dramatically. "For now."

AMONG WOLVES
A Shepherd and Fox Thriller

They were promised a simple job. Now they're fighting for their lives.

When a so-called "easy op" to protect business tycoon Drake Cryer on a shady deal goes horribly wrong, former Delta Force operative Shepherd and his top-notch partner Lucky are faced with a situation that's quickly spiraling into chaos. The pair are catapulted into a deadly mission to escape the clutches of a vicious Russian warlord.

Forced to team up with the infamous Darcy Brothers—a legendary mercenary duo with an uncanny ability to cheat death—Shepherd and Lucky must push their skills to the brink if they want to get out alive.

But they're stranded deep in hostile territory. With a sinister extortion plot hanging over the head of the CEO they swore to protect, Shepherd and his team will need to dance with the devil as they carry out a cunning plan to escape the country in one piece.

Death lurks around every corner—because nowhere is safe when you're Among Wolves...

ABOUT THE AUTHORS

Brian Shea has spent most of his adult life in service to his country and local community. He honorably served as an officer in the U.S. Navy. In his civilian life, he reached the rank of Detective and accrued over eleven years of law enforcement experience between Texas and Connecticut. Somewhere in the mix he spent five years as a fifth-grade school teacher. Brian's myriad of life experience is woven into the tapestry of each character's design. He resides in New England and is blessed with an amazing wife and three beautiful daughters.

USA Today bestselling and Agatha, Anthony, Barry, and Macavity Award Finalist Kristi Belcamino writes dark mysteries about fierce women seeking justice. She is a crime fiction writer, cops beat reporter, and Italian mama who also bakes a tasty biscotti. In her former life, as an award-winning crime reporter at newspapers in California, she flew over Big Sur in an FA-18 jet with the Blue Angels, raced a Dodge Viper at Laguna Seca, and attended barbecues at the morgue. Belcamino has written and reported about many high-profile cases including the Laci Peterson murder and Chandra Levy's disappearance. She has appeared on Inside Edition and her work has appeared in the New York Times, Writer's Digest, Miami Herald, San Jose Mercury News, and Chicago Tribune.

Printed in the United States
by Baker & Taylor Publisher Services